# DR. ANDROMEDA FALLOUT

PART 2

RAY THORNE

Dedicated to all those who I love and who
have supported me over the years . . . and to
those who have inspired me since I was a little
kid.

*Introduction*

After Allison Finkle had worked for the Omega Corporation and lost both her hands in the process, she went back into the world a changed human being. Due to the horrendous treatment she received from the Omega Corporation, her diabolical situation with the seedy John M., and the death of her friend Mia, Allison Finkle had transformed into Dr. Andromeda Fallout . . . a glowing-with-radioactivity-eyed, metal-handed force with plans . . . plans to work on neutralizing radiation as a result of nuclear fallout. Her plans did not stop there, however. Andromeda, with the help of her dog assistant named Turd, had more obstacles to overcome in the seemingly postapocalyptic new world order in which she lived. In balancing the fight between being the kindhearted and loving person she truly is and her propensity to become a destructive entity, Dr. Andromeda Fallout moves forward . . .

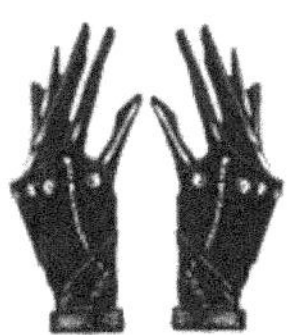

The bright morning sunlight came down through the front window of Dr. Andromeda Fallout's living room and onto her face as she lay fast asleep on the couch with her dog, Turd, snuggled in her arms. She slowly opened her eyes as the rays of the sun pierced her eyelids. With a little waking sniff, while wiping some drool from her cheek, she raised herself up to sit on the couch and yawned. Turd quickly opened his eyes and looked up at the woman who sat there rubbing her face, her golden-blond hair in a big, messy heap on her head.

"Good morning, Turd," said Andromeda sleepily. "Merry Christmas to you, and goodwill toward men."

"Peace and goodwill, Doc," laughed Turd as he stretched his limbs. "I slept so dang hard."

"After you go to the bathroom outside and we finish breakfast," said Andromeda, "we should open presents or something."

Turd barked, jumped excitedly onto the floor, and rushed to the front door. Andromeda sighed, rose to her feet, and stretched with a groan.

"Okay, okay, Turd," she chuckled. "I'm coming."

After Turd had finished his morning "duties" outside, the two went into the kitchen and ate breakfast. Andromeda made pancakes, and both of them hungrily cleaned their plates. They then opened the Christmas presents Andromeda had managed to sneak in the night before while Turd was asleep. She hadn't been able to buy much, given she shopped at the last minute, but she was able to use some extra funds from her tenure at the Omega Corporation, and Turd admired the warm dog sweater she got for him.

"Remember, Turd," said Andromeda, "tonight we have dinner at Mark's Bar with Mark and Audrey."

"Yeah! That will be fun!" said Turd excitedly. "I know they said not to bring anything, but do you think we still should?"

"Of course," replied Andromeda. "I'll make some cookies or something."

Andromeda went from the colorful tree, where the two were sitting, to the radio and placed a Nat King Cole Christmas vinyl on the record player before heading to the bathroom to get ready for the day. In the bathroom, she looked at her eyes in the mirror. They were still a fluorescent yellow.

"They don't appear to be getting any better," she murmured to herself in annoyance. "Glad I can still see just fine, but what a nuisance being the only human being in town with glowing eyeballs and indestructible metal hands."

Andromeda finished getting her face and hair ready for the day, although somewhat clumsily, since she was still getting used to her prostheses, and returned to the living room, where Turd sat watching the television.

"I wonder how the battery on your vocal collar is holding up," she said to the animal, kneeling next to him and checking the black box on Turd's collar.

"Appears to be okay," replied Turd.

"I think, if I recall when I first made the device, that it is supposed to beep when it is getting low on power," Andromeda continued. "But yes, it appears to be in good working order."

She patted Turd's head and went to the kitchen to start making a batch of cookies for the event later that evening. It was a pretty basic sugar cookie recipe, but it brought her all the way back to some very young childhood memories with her family, and the smell was something she adored.

Once the cookies were baked and put into the freezer to harden the icing, Andromeda and Turd decided to go out for a walk in the beautiful winter weather.

They admired the way the snow reflected the sunlight in an array of sparkles as they walked. Turd hopped around in the snow happily, even though it was deep enough to reach his chin. As they walked toward town, they came upon the used car dealership just on its outskirts. Andromeda encouraged Turd to join her in looking at the cars in the lot. Each car had a light blanket of snow over it, but they wiped them off as they moved from one to the next. Andromeda wished her VW Beetle hadn't been destroyed in the Omega Corporation explosion, so she decided to look around and see if there was a replacement in her price range.

"What about this car that is shaped like a big box?" asked Turd, sniffing a vehicle across from Andromeda.

"That Volvo?" she smiled, walking up to Turd and the car. "Maybe . . . Not a bad idea, they run for forever."

Suddenly a vehicle caught the corner of Andromeda's eye. She turned to look and saw a bit of red paint underneath a big, round mound of snow.

"Hm," said Andromeda, quickly walking over to the mound of snow. "Is this what I think it is?"

Turd pranced to her side. "What is it?" he asked.

"If my assumption is correct . . ." explained Andromeda, wiping the snow off the vehicle, "I think this is a . . ."

The snow was cleared and the round, iconic shape of a used VW Beetle stood before them. Its sharp red color flashed in the sunlight.

"It looks like an insect or something," muttered Turd.

"It's a Beetle!" exclaimed Andromeda, excitedly clapping her hands together with a loud clunk. "How beautiful!"

"I poop things bigger than that," said Turd bluntly.

"Gross," retorted Andromeda. "But anyway, isn't it so pretty? I love it!"

"I guess," mumbled Turd. "But you're so tall, Doc. No offense, but aren't you too big for a car that size?"

"These cars play a major trick on one's perception," said Andromeda. "There's more room in them than you'd think. I miss my last one."

"So your last one got the insecticide treatment when Omega exploded?" laughed Turd.

"Yes, Turd," replied Andromeda, somewhat dramatically. "I wish the dealership was open today. But of course, it is closed because it's Christmas Day."

"Do you need a car soon?" asked Turd.

"Yes," replied Andromeda. "I want to try out those capsules we were working on the other day in the lab—you know, the ones for eliminating radiation levels from fallout—in the area where Omega exploded. I'm not walking that many miles in the snow again. If we need to make a quick getaway, it would be better in a car than on foot."

"Very true," agreed Turd.

Andromeda sighed happily and carefully rubbed her mitten-covered hand over the fender of the car.

"I think I have enough money for you," she whispered to the Beetle.

Turd rolled his eyes at Andromeda's talking to a car as if it were alive.

"If the authorities wound up chasing us down, should they catch us on the site, especially in the snow," said Turd, "I don't think we could make much of a getaway in a little fart like that."

"It's not a little fart," retorted Andromeda. "These cars are little tanks in the snow. Plus . . ."

"Plus what?" asked Turd.

"When I'm finished with it," she continued, "they won't be following us for very long."

Turd looked questioningly into Andromeda's eyes. A sly grin crossed a corner of her mouth, and Turd began to grimace in response.

"So, Doc," said Turd. "You got a plan?"

"I always have a plan cooking," replied Andromeda. "You should know that by now, my darling Turd."

A car drove up into the lot and a man got out. Andromeda and Turd casually walked up to him.

"Sorry," said the man. "We are closed, but I had to stop by the office to grab something. Did you need any help?"

"I wanted to inquire about the VW over there," asked Andromeda, pointing toward the automobile.

"Got ya," replied the man. "Fairly low miles, no issues that I know of. We inspected it in our maintenance garage, and it checked out. We had a light blue one too, but a lady bought it yesterday before closing."

"I want it," said Andromeda, with a crazed, wide-eyed look on her face. "If you can help me out, even though you are closed, I'll take it off your hands right now."

The man paused for a moment, staring at the tall lady and her dog.

"All right, come on in." He sighed. "No haggling, you understand?"

"Nope," said Andromeda, smiling down at Turd. "Thank you, sir!"

The three figures walked into the dealership office.


"It drives rather nicely," said Turd from the passenger seat of the car as Andromeda excitedly drove the Beetle back to the house.

The little car made its typical buzzing engine noise as they rolled along.

"I love the interior on this one," she said, rubbing the dashboard. She turned the car in to her driveway and drove into the garage.

"We left the house to go for a walk," continued Turd, "and came back with a new car. How exciting!"

Andromeda rubbed the top of Turd's head before she got out to open the passenger-side door to let him out. The dog hopped out and instantly ran toward the front lawn and lifted his leg.

"Thank you for not pissing in the new car," she said, chuckling.

"Once you turned the heater on," sighed Turd, "I *had* to go."

Andromeda laughed as she closed the garage door. "After dinner tonight at Mark's bar," she said, "I'll show you some of the things we have to do to the car so we can maybe get to the Omega site before New Year's."

"Okay, cool," muttered Turd enthusiastically. "Another mission awaits us!"

Later that evening, the sun had set and the moon rose up over the white, snow-covered landscape that surrounded the small town.

Andromeda and Turd got themselves bundled up to go out for dinner at Mark's. After taking the tray of cookies from the refrigerator, they hopped into the Beetle and started the engine. As they slowly drove over the icy streets, Andromeda began to think about her plan to test out her experiment on the Omega disaster site.

"I think I will start mapping out the course of action tonight, after dinner," Andromeda said to Turd, holding the steering wheel tightly as she navigated the slippery street. "And what we need to do to the car for the getaway, should that complication arise."

"What do you have in mind so far?" asked Turd, admiring the new Christmas sweater that adorned him.

"We should do it under the cover of night," replied Andromeda. "And take the back road behind the big field that goes for most of the drive to the site. I've driven that route once before, when the main road was blocked off for construction when I worked there."

Turd listened intently.

"That route has a lot of tree cover as well, in case anything or anyone could spot us from above in the sky," continued Andromeda, "so we can remain hidden pretty well."

"Won't there be some form of security watch around the whole area though?" interrupted Turd.

"Possibly," replied Andromeda. "However, it is still a fairly fresh disaster site, and I don't think they'll be too well guarded yet, since it happened out in the middle of nowhere in the dead of winter. They will have the main road blocked off to traffic for sure, but they may not have it as well guarded yet on the back road. That is . . . if we can beat the security team to it before they send in their full crew of responders, which will be in the next week or so."

"What makes you think they won't have the back road as well guarded?" asked Turd.

"Because the radiation levels will be dangerous to human traffic and they don't have a full task force in the area yet," answered Andromeda. "I saw it on the news earlier. They, at the moment, are just asking civilians to stay as far away as possible. If they don't have a full task force to handle the area, they won't have very many willing police or other security to guard it."

"So what about us?" Turd continued. "How will we be able to handle the area if we are mere life forms? Won't the radiation levels be too dangerous for us as well?"

"That's where those capsules we made come into play," she replied. "If we can gown up for the basic protection needed against radiation, I can devise a few upgrades for the Beetle so we won't have to get too close."

"Like projecting them from the car?" asked Turd.

"Yes! Very good, Turd," answered Andromeda excitedly. "We need to put wireless detonators on the capsules so they will not ignite until long after they are projected from the Beetle. Then, once we are a safe distance away, we can detonate them from a controller in the car!"

"What about the guards?" asked Turd. "What do we do if they stop us before we get to where we need to be?"

"Ever heard of a roofie?" replied Andromeda.

"No," answered Turd.

"Well," continued Andromeda, "roofie is the nickname given to a drug called Rohypnol. It causes amnesia in those who ingest it."

"Amnesia?" asked Turd, confused.

"Amnesia is a partial or total loss of memory," replied Andromeda. "If we can create a smoke screen that can be sprayed from the car into the surrounding area, we can load the smoke compound with a heavy dosage of Rohypnol. That, combined with a strong sedative, should not only knock out whoever tries to stop us from getting through a barricade but also leave them with total memory loss of us even having been there in the first place."

"So basically, put them all to sleep," said Turd. "And when they wake up, they won't remember anything . . . the car, us, anything?"

"Exactly!" exclaimed Andromeda.

"Okay, cool," said Turd with a shrug. He looked out the car window.

"I should be able to make the chemicals needed in the lab," continued Andromeda, pulling the car into the parking lot of Mark's Bar. "This way, no one will get hurt during the mission, and I'll have the results of the experiment . . . and no one will know who actually performed this major feat! At this moment, we need to lie low and not expose ourselves. The government will immediately get involved with me, and I want nothing to do with our regime right now. I don't want this discovery to fall into the wrong hands. Not after what happened to me and those around me."

"We will get it done," smiled Turd. "It'll be great . . . Dr. Andromeda Fallout!"

"Okay, okay," laughed Andromeda, shutting the car off and opening her door. "We have to see the results first. Now let's go get some dinner."

Turd howled comically in response as the two walked from the car and into Mark's Bar.

Mark's Bar was decorated with a lot of holiday decorations and colorful lights hanging all around the main room that housed the tables. Andromeda and Turd admired the sight as they entered the room. Audrey, Mark's assistant at the bar and store, greeted them.

"Merry Christmas!" Audrey exclaimed. "So glad you two could make it!"

Andromeda smiled and held out the tray of cookies they had brought.

"You didn't have to bring anything," said Audrey kindly. "Thank you, these look delicious!"

Mark walked up to the group from behind the bar, where he finished laying out a buffet table of food.

"I do buffet for you guy," he said in his broken English. "We have one or two more people coming, so we start soon."

"That'll be wonderful." Andromeda thanked him while taking off her coat, which Audrey took to hang up. "Who else is coming?" she asked.

"Audrey, who else come?" Mark asked Audrey.

"My friend Avory Pringle, and that Betty," replied Audrey.

At that moment, a black cat leapt onto a table nearby, and Audrey quickly glanced over at it.

"Oh! And you too, Phineas," smiled Audrey at the cat.

"I'm afraid I don't know them," said Andromeda. "Being new in town and all."

"Yeah, that right," said Mark, winking at her.

Andromeda nervously smiled back at Mark. She had the growing feeling that Mark knew about her past for some reason, but she decided to keep up the status quo about her identity.

Audrey coaxed the guests over to a table and asked them if they wanted anything to drink. Andromeda and Turd requested eggnog, so Audrey went to retrieve some. That was when the door burst open and two figures came into the room from the snow that had begun to pick up outside.

The figures were bundled up from head to toe and covered in snow. One figure was tall, a little shorter than Andromeda, and the other was shorter, around average height, like Audrey.

"*Happy Christmas!*" boomed the voice of the tall figure, almost making the windows rattle.

"Oh, hi, Betty!" said Mark.

"Hello, Betty," murmured Audrey.

Andromeda and Turd watched as the two figures removed their snow-covered garments. The taller one, Betty, had dark brown hair and big blue eyes. The smaller figure took their hat off and exposed a fluffy mass of blue hair with a large pink streak in the bangs. It was Avory Pringle, and her lips were shivering while her eyes glared up from under her hair somewhat menacingly.

"And hello, Avory," greeted Audrey kindly. "Glad you made it!"

"There is snow . . ." murmured Avory, with a long exhale, "everywhere."

"There sure is!" exclaimed Betty, slapping Avory on the back.

Avory closed her eyes and exhaled again in annoyance.

Audrey invited them farther into the room to introduce Avory and Betty to the two sitting at the table.

"Nice to meet you both," said Andromeda sweetly.

"Nice to meet you, too," said Avory in a monotone voice—her voice rarely reached anything other than a monotone.

"Don't mind her," boomed Betty. "She takes everything so seriously!"

"Did I ask you to explain my existence?" Avory asked Betty.

"Oh, come on, Avory," Betty continued to boom. "Lighten up! It's Christmas!"

"I despise Christmas," said Avory as she looked up wide-eyed into Betty's face.

Andromeda's mouth fell open in shock. "I love Christmas," she said. "It's my favorite time of the year."

"At least you have a favorite time of the year," grumbled Avory, once again very monotone, as she suddenly turned and walked out of Andromeda's view and sat at the table next to them.

Andromeda and Turd looked at each other, very confused.

"Don't mind her," exclaimed Betty. "She is fine once you get to know her."

"Okay! Don't have time for this," interrupted Mark. "Food gonna go bad if you guy don't go get some!"

The entire group walked over to the bar buffet to help themselves, and once they were done, they all sat back down at tables next to each other. As they ate, they began to converse with one another.

"So, what's with the black metal gloves?" Avory asked Andromeda bluntly.

Andromeda suddenly realized that she had totally forgotten about her hands being exposed. So she quickly thought over what to say.

"They . . . uh . . ." she stammered. "They aren't gloves. They are my real hands."

"Oh wow, really?" asked Avory.

The others stared at Andromeda questioningly while Turd began to wince.

"Yes," answered Andromeda, after a pause. "I had an accident a while back."

"Why are your eyes all a bright yellow?" asked Betty.

"Birth defect," stammered Andromeda.

"Come on, guys," interjected Audrey. "Leave her alone. Wouldn't you feel awkward if everyone asked you about your physical appearance?"

"No," cut in Betty. "I love attention!"

"Didn't your parents teach you not to draw attention to yourself?" laughed Audrey.

"Nope," chuckled Betty.

"I wouldn't raise my kids like that," murmured Avory, staring seriously at Betty.

"This has got to be one of the goofiest conversations to have over Christmas dinner," said Turd laughingly.

"It's okay," chuckled Andromeda. "It's something I've had to continue to get used to. No worries."

Everyone looked down at their plates and continued to eat their meal.

"So," started Andromeda. "How do you all know one another?"

Audrey answered for the lot. "We are all in a musical rock group that Mark started a while back," she replied. "Mark plays organ and keyboard bass, Avory is our lead guitarist, Betty helps with stage setup, Phineas sings, and I play rhythm guitar."

"Wait, what?" asked Andromeda. "The cat sings?"

"Yes," said the cat suddenly.

Andromeda looked up in surprise—she didn't know that the cat could speak! After all, he hadn't spoken a word to anyone up until this point during the party.

"Yes," continued Phineas. "I can talk. Let's just say it's a special gift I received upon birth."

"He's a supernatural cat," said Audrey. "He is an anomaly. All of us are an anomaly in one way or another."

Turd glared at Phineas. "And I need a collar in order to speak," he murmured. Andromeda patted his head understandingly.

"I used to play the piano," said Andromeda with a sigh. "But after my accident, I lost the ability to play."

Audrey looked at her sadly. "I'm so sorry," she whispered. "Maybe you can learn to play again?"

"We shall see," answered Andromeda. "I'm not one to give up very easily."

"That is for sure!" exclaimed Turd, smiling. "You never know what things are up Dr. Andromeda's sleeve!"

"You're a doctor?" asked Avory, cramming a spoonful of stuffing into her mouth.

"Yes," replied Andromeda. "Of nuclear physics, among other things."

"That's pretty dope," said Avory, her cheeks bloated with food. "Cool to meet an egghead like yourself."

"Oh my word," groaned Audrey, rolling her eyes.

"It's okay," laughed Andromeda. "I am a bit of an egghead, I guess."

"And I am the walrus!" exclaimed Turd.

"Beatle lyrics," said Avory, nodding from under the hair over her eyes. "Very good reference. It's not a perfect lyrical reference, but a good one nonetheless."

After another half hour of random chitchat, the group finished their plates, sat back in their chairs, and sighed in contentment. Mark and Audrey stood up, began to clear the dishes from the table, and offered dessert and after-dinner drink specialties. It had been a wonderful time for Andromeda and Turd, as well as the others. They were all very happy to have met one another and even made plans to get together again in the future.

Once the guests had gathered their coats, they went out into the cold of the night and separated. Mark and Audrey waved at them from the bar doorway.

"I'm glad that went well," said Audrey, wrapping her arm around Mark. "You did a wonderful job on the buffet setup."

"Thanks." Mark smiled. "You did wonderful job on setup too."

The couple embraced as they quickly planted a kiss on each other's lips.

Andromeda and Turd walked across the parking lot toward her vehicle. "It was so nice to be invited to that," said Andromeda. She and Turd got into the VW Beetle. "They seemed to enjoy the cookies we brought, too."

"It has been a very good Christmas," agreed Turd. "Thank you for welcoming me into your life, Doc."

Andromeda smiled and hugged the animal sitting in the passenger seat. "Thank you for coming into it," she said, almost shedding a tear of happiness. "We got this Turd . . . we got this."

Later that night Dr. Andromeda stood out in the garage, scratching her head while looking at the VW Beetle. Its body was dripping with water as the ice melted off it, since the car had sat in the elements for a while in the parking lot at Mark's Bar earlier.

*Let's see,* thought Andromeda to herself, rubbing her chin. *I'll need to manufacture some valves for the smoke screen in both the front and back so that they can be opened from inside the cabin. The trunk can hold the tank containing the smokescreen fluid, and that will need a pump to pressurize the liquid through the tubes to the valves located at the front and back bumpers. Through the pressure of the pump, and the chemical mixture, it should create a large enough smokescreen.*

*I just need to make sure that the Rohypnol mixed with some form of strong sedative, like chloroform, will work and that the cloud dosage when inhaled isn't too strong. Strong enough to knock out anyone attempting to stop the experiment, but not to the extent of being lethal. The potency of the mixture will mostly dissipate into the air, since placing it in a smoke screen isn't an exact dosage for whoever inhales it, but I guess that is a chance I will have to take.*

Andromeda grinned and the chuckled slyly as she concluded her thoughts. She quickly walked from the garage and into the house, where Turd lay sprawled out and snoring on the couch. She was careful not to wake him as she tiptoed past and while opening the secret island-counter door in the floor leading to the basement laboratory. Once settled at her desk in the lab, she began to draw up a diagram for the Beetle that included all the details she had brought to her own attention while in the garage.

As she made notes on the diagram, Andromeda noticed that she was becoming more accustomed to her metal hands. "Each and every day," she said to herself, "you're getting better and better with these things. It's been a rough patch here, but you are doing great. You . . . are . . . doing . . . *great!*"

For hours into the night, Andromeda worked on building the devices she needed to put into the car to create the smoke screen mechanism, as well as a gun to project the antiradiation capsules into the fallout site. The gun she concocted was basically a potato cannon with a chamber for hairspray gas and a double-ignition electronic lighter as its firing power. It was something that could fire the capsules at a longer range and not damage them, as gunpowder would have, she concluded.

The capsules didn't weigh very much, no more than a potato, so it would have plenty of firing power for the job. She figured the velocity range of the cannon was around two hundred meters, or around six hundred and fifty-six feet, and that seemed close enough, since the detonation radius of each capsule was around one hundred yards. If she were to fire the capsules in succession over half a mile as she drove, that should clear up most of the radiation in the area.

Andromeda wanted everything to be concealed in a way so as not to cause any unwanted attention when she was out and about driving. After she had the parts put together and ready to be installed in the Beetle, she brought the load up the stairs, through the house, and into the garage. Andromeda was exhausted by this point, since she hadn't slept since the day before, but her drive to complete this build kept her awake.

As the sun began to show itself over the horizon, she made the finishing touches on the installation. Andromeda stood back and sighed with pride at her accomplishment. She went back into the house to wake Turd, who was still passed out on the couch.

"Wake up, Turd!" she exclaimed excitedly. "Come see what I did to the car last night!"

Turd reluctantly dragged himself upright, and after letting the cobwebs from sleep clear, he hopped off the couch and followed Andromeda into the garage. "The car looks the same as it did yesterday," he mumbled as he got his first glimpse of the day at the automobile.

"What's the big deal?"

"Take a closer look, and I'll explain," answered Andromeda jovially.

She proceeded first to show the dog the cockpit of the car, where two small levers stuck out from under the driver's side and the passenger's side of the console. "These levers control the valve openings at the front and back of the vehicle," she explained. "The driver's-side lever controls the front valve, and the passenger's side controls the back one. You'll be in charge of the back valve, of course. The wireless detonator for the antiradiation capsules is located in the glove compartment."

"Very nice," yawned Turd. "Where does the smoke come from?"

"I'll show you." Andromeda led him to the trunk of the car. Opening the trunk hatch revealed a large tank with a pump attached to it. The whole setup filled most of the trunk space. Tubes ran from the tank into the pump, and from there into a small hole located at the back of the rear seats.

"The chemical mixture for the smoke screen travels from the tank, into the pump, and through those tubes to the valve openings," she explained. "Then *poof!* Anyone attempting to stop us will be met by a thick cloud of smoke and will end up falling fast asleep in a matter of seconds. That is my hope, anyway."

"Excellent work, Doc! What about the thing to project the capsules onto the site?"

"I'll have you point the cannon I made from the passenger window," she replied. "I'll pull the trigger from the driver's side."

"You've thought about everything!" Turd shouted.

Andromeda smiled and patted the dog's head. They walked back into the house and sat down on the couch, where Andromeda discovered that she could barely keep her eyes open.

"You haven't slept since yesterday, have you?" asked Turd.

"No, but I'm all right," replied Andromeda with a yawn. "I'm too excited to sleep."

Turd looked at her questioningly. After a pause, Andromeda's head fell back against the couch as she fell into a deep sleep. Turd snickered, hopped off the couch, and walked into the kitchen to find something to eat.

When Andromeda awoke, she looked up at the clock on the wall and found that she had slept most of the day away. It was now evening, and the sun had set. She sat up with a groan and stretched her aching body. After a long, dull moment of staring at the Christmas tree in a daze, she got herself off the couch and into the kitchen, where Turd was sitting at the table.

"You're up, Sleeping Beauty!" he said with a smile.

"Sure am," Andromeda replied. "I can't believe I slept all day."

"You needed it," said Turd. "You did a lot of stuff to the car last night!"

"True," she replied, pulling a ginger ale from the fridge. "I think we should try the experimental mission tonight. Get it out of the way in the post-Christmas doldrums between the holiday and New Year's. With everyone sitting at home, off the roads, sleeping off their parties, we can take advantage of the lack of traffic around places like the Omega disaster site."

"Great idea, Doc!" exclaimed Turd. "No one would suspect us. Any attention would be on the more Neapolitan areas."

"I think you mean *metropolitan*, Turd," laughed Andromeda. "We don't live in Naples, and we aren't ice cream."

"I love ice cream!" barked Turd.

Andromeda rolled her eyes and laughed as she walked out of the kitchen and into her bedroom. She looked through the closet to find her snowsuit in preparation for the mission. Turd joined her in the room, and the two discussed what they would need to complete the preparations. They would have to bundle up warmly in case they needed to leave the vehicle for any reason, retrieve radiation suits, and grab a Geiger counter.

The suits and Geiger counter were in the laboratory, so they went down the secret stairs to get them. As they zipped up their suits, the finishing touches were complete. They were now ready to load the antiradiation capsules and the cannon into the Beetle.

Dr. Andromeda and Turd sat silently in the car as she started its engine. They looked cautiously at each other as the vehicle sat idling and breathed in deep.

"All right," she said with a sigh. "Here we go."

Turd nodded nervously in response.

The garage door opened and cold air flooded in. It was snowing fairly heavily as the car backed down the driveway. Andromeda pulled the vehicle onto the street and drove into the swirling clouds of snow. As the lights of the houses faded into the rearview mirror, the darkness in front of the car loomed large. Most of the moonlight was shaded by cloud cover, so it made seeing through the windshield rather difficult.

Andromeda hoped that by the time they reached the countryside, where their destination was, the weather would clear up a bit. She felt the surge of an almost crazed determination come over her... the overwhelming feeling she had felt when she destroyed the Omega building, when she killed the drunk in the alleyway, and when she destroyed John M. She stared forward, not blinking. Turd had begun to recognize this look, the look she would get in her yellow eyes if something triggered her in some way. He noticed it at the car dealership when she talked to the salesman, when she reminisced at home, and other times when they worked together in the lab. It was a mixture of blankness, anger, and utter determination all in one stare. Once the look came, it was something you couldn't snap her out of.

Turd didn't question Dr. Andromeda when these moments came over her, since he figured it was due to some form of posttraumatic stress or some other mental quirk. Despite his sometimes-uneasy feeling about these moments, he was very happy to be in her family. He also concluded that he needn't be afraid of her, since he was on her side . . . but whoever was not . . . he pitied them.

The Beetle zoomed on steadily through the snowy streets. There was not another vehicle in sight as they made their way into the countryside. The snowfall, as Andromeda had hoped, had begun to lessen, though the snow-covered fields stood on either side of the road in massive sheets of white. They came to the fork in the road that split the main road and the back road. Andromeda turned onto the back road and gunned the little vehicle through the snow that had drifted over the street.

"We're almost there, Turd," she said quietly yet sternly. Turd nervously nodded in response.

They arrived at the part of the road that had a lot of tree cover. What remained of the moon's light was now completely gone from view, and an eerie silence filled the air. All that could be heard was the buzzing of the Beetle's engine. As they drove through the tunnel of trees, they reached a blockade sign that warned drivers to turn around. Andromeda smiled somewhat menacingly, with a sly glint in her eyes. She slammed the gas pedal to the floor and the car lurched forward. Turd looked up at the doctor and then quickly at the blockade sign.

"Hold on to your butt, Turd!" cried Andromeda, starting to laugh.

The dog frantically looked back and forth from her to the blockade as it drew closer and closer with every split second. "Oh, shit!" he howled.

The Beetle smashed through the blockade sign, sending shards of wood and reflector tape everywhere. Andromeda looked into the rearview mirror and saw red and blue lights begin to flash behind them. It was a police cruiser.

"Son of a bitch," she muttered under her breath. "We've got company." She punched the gas pedal again, sending the car skidding on the ice around a bend in the road. The police cruiser came close to hitting them as it slid sideways, bumping into a snowbank on the side of the street before moving forward.

"Get the cannon ready by the window," ordered Andromeda to Turd. "It looks like we only have one pursuer at the moment. I can try and shake them."

Turd pushed the nose of the cannon against the window next to him. Andromeda pulled a can of hairspray out from the console between them.

"Get the Geiger counter turned on," she further ordered. "Once it is switched on, it will begin to tick extremely fast. The ticking speed will tell us just how heavy the amounts of radiation are in the area. It will be a strong reading, I presume, and we need to know that so we will know where we need to be to start firing the capsules."

Turd nodded in understanding and urgently reached his muzzle into the back seat, where the Geiger counter sat. He clicked the switch on with his teeth, and the machine started ticking very fast.

"Okay," continued Andromeda. "We need to move quickly when I open your window. Keep your face and radiation mask low from the window."

"Okay, Doc," answered Turd.

As the car reached the outskirts of the field where the disaster had happened, Andromeda opened the passenger window. Turd loaded a capsule into the barrel of the cannon. Andromeda sprayed the hairspray gases into the firing chamber and closed its compartment door. Upon pushing the igniter button, the cannon let out a loud boom that sent a capsule flying into the sky over the field. The police cruiser slammed on its brakes and slid into a ditch on the side of the road.

"Shots fired!" came a voice from a loudspeaker on the police cruiser.

Andromeda and Turd quickly, and with great precision, managed to fire off the capsules one by one as they sped onward next to the field. After they had fired all of them, Andromeda spun the car around and headed back the way they had come. They could see another set of flashing lights appear and stop next to the cruiser parked in the ditch ahead of them.

"Keep your head down," said Andromeda, "in case they start shooting at us. If they don't, I have an idea. Just stay down." Turd whimpered in response.

Andromeda slowed down the car and came to a stop by the police cruisers. Two officers, not wearing much protection against the radiation levels in the area, walked up next to her window and began banging on it. She rolled down her window.

"Please officers," she began to shout. "Get back in your cars! You aren't wearing the protective gear needed! The radiation levels here will kill you!"

"Get out of the car!" screamed one of the officers.

"I will get out," she answered. "Once we are safely past the blockade sign that I smashed back there!"

After a short pause, the two officers looked at the suited-up woman in the car and then at each other.

"I'm not kidding!" Andromeda exclaimed. "You are going to die soon if you stay here!"

The officers rushed to their vehicles as Andromeda pulled forward. She floored the car down the road and out of the field area as the police cruisers followed close behind her.

"Good job, Turd," said Andromeda as she drove into the tree tunnel. "Stay down. There is one more little trick to try once we are safely away and before we detonate the capsules in the area. Be ready with your smokescreen lever."

"You got it, Doc," answered Turd.

The Beetle reached the site of the smashed blockade sign and stopped. The two police cruisers pulled up behind it, and the officers got out. They didn't seem as frenetic as they were before, since they had begun to understand that the woman in the red VW seemed to know what she was talking about and that she had pulled over like she had promised. They, this time, knocked a bit more gently on the window. Andromeda politely rolled it down.

"Okay, miss," said one of the officers, removing his small radiation mask. "What the hell were you doing back there? What is this all about?"

"Yes," chimed in the other officer, removing his mask as well. "Why were you firing a gun in a blocked-off area? Not to mention smashing the blockade signage?"

Andromeda breathed in deeply as she thought, her fingers lying right next to the lever for the smokescreen by her knees. Turd pretended he was just an ordinary dog on the passenger seat, behaving clueless about everything even though he too was wearing a radiation suit. He sniffed around the lever to his smokescreen valve in preparation to use it, although very nonchalantly.

"It's like this," started Andromeda, as the officers shined a light into her eyes. "I was attempting an experiment, you see, in which . . ."

She pulled the smokescreen lever, as did Turd. An explosion of smoke and mist enveloped the area outside the car. The officers backed away from the car, coughing and choking. Andromeda rolled up her window and watched as the police officers began to struggle to stay on their feet. After a few moments, they fell to the ground motionless. She and the dog turned the valve levers off, and the smoke began to clear.

"Okay, Turd," said Andromeda. "I need to get them out of the cold and into their cars. I'll be right back."

Turd nodded as she got out and walked to the two bodies, which lay snoring on the ground.

"Well, at least you two are still breathing," said Andromeda. "I pity your wives or girlfriends if they have to listen to that kind of snoring when you sleep."

She carefully dragged each officer over to his respective cruiser. "Oh my word," she said, pushing a slumped-over officer into the driver's seat. "You're heavy! Must be your tactical gear."

Once both officers were in their vehicles, still passed out, Andromeda went back to the Beetle and sat down behind the wheel. "Okay, Turd," she said, opening the glove compartment containing the wireless detonator for the capsules. "Here's the moment of truth."

Turd covered his ears with his paws. Andromeda pressed the button on the detonator . . .

Nothing happened. Nothing but silence and darkness filled the air around them.

"Are you serious?" asked Andromeda. She began to push the detonator button over and over again. Turd sighed in despair.

Andromeda slammed the detonator down onto the console between them and placed a hand on her forehead. "All this work," she sighed. "And they won't flipping detonate!" Turd could see how upset she was, so he remained silent.

Suddenly a bright, colorful light flashed across the area from behind the car! The two looked behind them through the rear window in shock as an array of phosphorescent colors whirled around in a ghostly fashion over the fields. They looked at each other, stunned at the sight, and then locked their eyes on the scene.

"It's working!" exclaimed Andromeda.

After a series of constant flashes and a whirling of colors, Andromeda and Turd watched as the lights began to fizzle out. Once they all seemed to have disappeared, Andromeda started the car and turned it around to head back to the site.

"Why are we going back?" asked Turd.

"We need to see if the capsules worked," replied Andromeda. "Turn on the Geiger counter, please."

Turd flipped the switch on the counter. It began to tick in a slow, regular rhythm, not detecting any radiation. The two drove down the road by the field into which they had fired the capsules, and still the Geiger counter detected no radiation.

"It worked," said Andromeda with a sigh.

"You're a genius, Doc," whispered Turd. "This invention cannot fall into the wrong hands."

"I'm in control, Turd," continued Andromeda. "With this sort of power at my metal fingertips, I could control the outcomes of wars between whole countries."

Turd looked at her wide-eyed. He noticed that she was staring almost angrily into the windshield, gritting her teeth.

"I'm . . . in . . . control," she hissed, as a crazed look bathed her face and eyes.

"What are you going to do now?" asked Turd.

"We wait," Andromeda hissed unflinchingly. "We wait and see what happens when the responders come to test this area. They, at first, will be baffled by the fact that they can't detect radiation. Then they will want to investigate why. The Omega Corporation will want to know why. The government will want to know why. Everyone will want to know *why*."

Turd's eyes grew wider in concern as her voice began to grow louder and more crazed as she spoke.

"And what happens when people want to know *why*?" she continued, starting to giggle maniacally. "They will investigate *who* did this. When they find out *who* did this? They will force that *who* to work for them, or kill that *who*."

Turd whimpered.

"I need to beat them at their own game, Turd," said Andromeda, beginning to soften her voice and leaning back in her seat. "Once this gets out, I need to protect you and me."

"How will you beat them at their own game?" whispered Turd.

"I'll find a way," replied Andromeda. "Omega will be doing a job fair for the employees that were put out of work when the building was destroyed. I saw something about it on the news before Christmas. They plan to start it after New Year's."

"What does a job fair have to do with anything concerning you?" asked Turd.

"I want to get to the head, or heads, of that corporation," she continued. "If I can manage to stop them in their tracks or foil their attempts to build again near the town, that would be one less thing to worry about."

"So, I take it you have more things planned," said Turd. "You always have something up your sleeve, don't you?"

"Well, Turd," answered Andromeda, beginning to choke on her words, "I . . . I can't let what is going on continue to happen. This world is in a terrible spot. Our town is headed that way as well. If I can do something to change that, I will try."

"And the next step, in your opinion, is to continue to stop Omega from ever coming back?" asked the animal. "Is this a step in a plot to do anything bigger?"

"Everything in life is another step," she replied. "And I have a score to settle with that corporate entity. It is so large and powerful, and has such pull with the government, that I believe severely hurting them from within will be the first major step in getting the people to respond to the evil that is inherent in that place. To get the people to revolt against this system and realize that they can live in safety in the world in which they are being destroyed.

The next morning Andromeda awoke to the sounds of a blizzard as winds pounded against the windowpane of her bedroom. She sat up on the edge of the bed, yawned, and shivered as her bare feet reached the hardwood floor, which was very cold. She walked to the thermostat and turned it up, figuring that the temperature had dropped significantly during the night.

Turd lay snoring on the couch in the living room. After putting on a pot of coffee in the kitchen, Andromeda walked back to the living room and sat down in the chair next to the couch. She turned on the television and looked over at the Christmas tree. Its colorful lights radiated through the shade-filled room. Turd opened his eyes at the sound of the TV.

"Good morning, Doc," he said with a snort.

"Good morning to you," answered Andromeda. "I put some coffee on. Do you want some?"

"Coffee makes me fart," replied the animal. "I would rather not."

Andromeda giggled as she stood to retrieve a cup of coffee from the kitchen. After filling a cup and grabbing a box of cookies from the pantry, she sat back down in front of the TV. Turd was sitting up on the couch watching it as she tuned in to see a reporter talking on the screen.

"People of the local area," said the reporter, "a strange and exciting occurrence happened last night at the site of the Omega Corporation disaster . . ."

Andromeda and Turd glanced at each other quickly and smirked.

"Two police officers were found this morning," continued the reporter. "They were found drugged in their police cruisers near the blockade sign, which was smashed, just on the outskirts of the fallout area. When they were interrogated by the precinct about what had happened last night, they were unable to answer or remember anything.

"A witness who lives several miles from the back-country road near the site reported that last night, strange lights had appeared over the fallout site. At the time, they suspected UFO or extraterrestrial doings as the answer to the phenomenon. That was until this morning, when scientists from the city were called in by the police precinct to investigate the area. What they found was shocking!

"The dangerous levels of radiation in the area contaminated by the explosion earlier this month have disappeared! Never in the history of science has such a phenomenon occurred, and it cannot be explained. It has baffled the scientists involved. They have sent their findings to officials involved with both Omega and the government.

"We will update you with further reports once we know anything more . . ."

"Here we go," said Andromeda, rolling her eyes. "They're going to get involved." Turd nodded slowly at her.

"In other news today," started the reporter once again, "the Omega Corporation will be holding a job fair and banquet at the Harris Hotel this Saturday night, the thirty-first of December. It is for all past employees that who were put out of work after the destruction of the building they worked at—and for anyone interested in finding employment . . ."

Andromeda sighed in disgust at the TV.

"And this report just came in," said the reporter, in closing. "The Omega Corporation has decided to rebuild their location as soon as possible at the site where they were previously located, on the outskirts of town. So for any of you out of a job due to the incident before Christmas or searching for new employment, it looks like there will be opportunities to start the new year off right!"

"Son of a bitch!" exclaimed Andromeda. She launched herself out of her chair. "They're planning to rebuild here sooner than I thought! I should have left the damn fallout site as is and not fixed it with my discovery!"

Turd huffed and hopped down from the couch. "I'm hungry," he said. "I need sustenance."

Andromeda, after a moment of scowling at the television in extreme anger, sighed off her temper and smiled at the dog. "Okay," she said quietly. "Let's get some breakfast for you."

As Turd ate his breakfast, Andromeda sipped her coffee at the table across from him. "Let's go get you a bed today, Turd," she said. "We can go to Mark's Bar and General Store and get you one this afternoon. So you don't have to sleep on the couch."

"Okay, cool," answered the animal, his mouth full of food. "Can I put it in your room?"

"Of course," Andromeda replied. "It would probably be a good idea anyway, in case we ever end up under the gun with authorities associated with the Omega incident. If the house were to be raided or anything like that, we could get away together quickly through the bedroom window. The window is right next to the garage where the car is for a getaway. We have to watch ourselves more carefully now than ever, so having an escape plan is the best solution."

Turd agreed and finished his breakfast.

As the morning passed and the afternoon arrived, Andromeda and Turd put their winter gear on and hopped into the VW Beetle. They drove down the slippery streets toward town, the windshield wipers doing their best to clear the swirling snow from the windshield. Andromeda carefully maneuvered the vehicle over the snowdrifts that covered the road.

When the neon sign for Mark's Bar and General Store came into view, she pulled the vehicle into the parking lot, and the two got out. The parking lot had not been plowed yet, so Turd had to exert a lot of energy to hop through the snow that came up to his neck. Andromeda bent over and picked him up into her arms. Turd panted quite heavily as she trudged up to the front door of the storefront and opened it.

Upon entering the store, Andromeda set Turd down and wiped the snow from her coat while the dog shook the flakes from his body. They were greeted by Audrey, who seemed excited to see them. Andromeda, feeling very welcome, asked her if they had any dog beds for sale. Audrey waved them over to a back wall in the store and showed them the inventory. After only a few minutes of deciding, Turd chose a black bed with red velvet trim. The bed was soft and fluffy, a detail that Turd especially wanted. As they walked up to the counter to pay for the bed, a solitary figure dressed all in black walked through the store's door.

"Ugh," came a grumble, followed by a long and breathy sigh from the figure as they removed the scarf that covered their face. The face was that of Avory Pringle, the blue-haired girl Andromeda and Turd had met at the Christmas party. Her face quivered as she stood shivering in annoyance.

"Oh, hi, Avory," said Audrey from behind the counter. "What brings you in today?"

Avory stared seriously across the room from under the pink streak in her blue hair. "I have come for some chips and dip," she said. She sighed again. "I'm hungry."

Andromeda couldn't help but chuckle internally at the seriousness and silent demeanor with which Avory always acted and spoke. She watched as Audrey pointed Avory toward the aisle that contained the things she was after. Avory, hunched over, walked down the aisle and out of sight.

"She is so serious," whispered Andromeda to Audrey from across the counter. "I've never met anyone with her personality type."

Audrey giggled and wiped the white-blond hair from her forehead. "Yes, she is a trip," she smiled, stuffing the dog bed into a large bag. "A good trip . . . Although she can be ridiculously depressed all the time, she is a good trip nonetheless."

Andromeda took the bag from Audrey and looked down at Turd. "Here you go, Turd," she said, pointing to the bag. "You can now give the couch a break."

"Thanks, Doc," smiled Turd excitedly.

Avory walked up behind them, holding four bags of potato chips and two jars of French onion dip, as they turned to leave the store. "I need to ask you something," she said to Andromeda, suddenly. "Can I talk to you for a second?"

"Of course," answered Andromeda. "What's up?"

"Can I come over or meet up with you?" asked Avory. "It might take more than a second, actually."

"I suppose so," Andromeda replied. "I gather that it's important, isn't it?"

"Yes," said Avory, her round, brown eyes widening to the size of dinner plates. "It's very important, you see."

"Okay," smiled Andromeda, after a quizzical pause. "Stop by my place this afternoon, and we can talk over lunch."

Avory sighed as a tiny smile reached the edges of her mouth. "Thank you," she said. "That would be nice, or something."

Andromeda grinned and stepped away from the counter. "See you later this afternoon, then," she said, opening the door for Turd.

Avory stared, smiling, as the two left the store. Audrey, looking questioningly at Avory, took the chips and dip from her arms and scanned them at the register.

"What are you up to?" asked Audrey.

"Oh, nothing," stammered Avory, realizing she had begun to space out. "I just have a few questions for Andromeda."

"What about?" continued Audrey, with one eyebrow raised in question.

"I'm going to ask her about getting a job at Omega," said Avory. "You see her hands? She totally worked there. We have a ton of people around town with robotic limbs that worked for that place . . . and I need a job. Maybe she can give me some information about the place once it is rebuilt here in town."

Audrey seemed puzzled. "What about the band?" she asked, taking a twenty-dollar bill from Avory and placing it in the till.

"I am just going to see what it entails to work there," replied Avory. "I'm not leaving the band. I just want to get some information."

"If you do get a job there," mumbled Audrey as she closed the till and handed Avory her change, "keep your limbs. You don't want to be unable to play guitar anymore, do you?"

"Like I said, Audrey," retorted Avory, with a loud exhale, "I'm just asking for information from her."

Audrey put her hands in the air and nodded. "I know, I know," she said. "Sorry to pry."

Avory took her bagged items from Audrey. "It's okay, Audrey," she grinned. "It'll be okay."

Avory walked over to the door and exited the store. Audrey remained silent behind the counter and sighed. "I wonder what she is up to," she murmured to herself.

The doorbell sounded in Andromeda's home, so she went to the door to answer it. She was met by Avory Pringle, who had arrived for lunch, standing on the front stoop. Andromeda welcomed her into the house and made Avory a cup of tea to warm herself, since the girl was shivering from the cold outdoors.

"So, what was it exactly that you wanted to see me about?" asked Andromeda as she sat down on the couch across from Avory.

Avory sat slouched in the chair, warming her hands over the cup of tea. "I just wanted to ask you a few questions, actually," she murmured.

"Okay, shoot," said Andromeda.

Avory sat up and leaned forward in her chair. "You worked for the Omega Corporation, didn't you?" she asked.

Andromeda paused in silence, her eyes darting at the question. "Y-yes," she hesitated. "Why do you want to know?"

"Because I may be looking into getting a job there," continued Avory. "I heard that they will be rebuilding soon—it said so on the news this morning—and they will be holding a job fair this Saturday."

"No!" exclaimed Andromeda, suddenly trembling. "Don't do it!"

"Why not?" asked Avory, with a sly glint in her eyes.

"Well, I might as well tell you," said Andromeda while Turd stared at her as he chewed on a dog toy.

Avory listened quietly and intently.

"Yes, I worked for the Omega Corporation," said Andromeda. "I worked there most of the summer and into the winter, up until around Christmas. It was a hellhole of a place to be working for. They are physically abusive toward their employees. If you don't perform to their standards, they cut off whichever limb they see as a cause of your not being up to par with the work. They call these amputations 'corrections.' There were many workers that received corrections. I'm sure you've seen some of them around town."

"So they cut off limbs and are physically abusive," said Avory, sipping her tea. "Anything else?"

Andromeda sat back and brushed the messy blond hair from her forehead. "The company also has strong connections with the government, so they can get away with murder if they see fit. The government allows them to do more than most companies that I know of.

"My friend Mia, who I had met at Omega, had both her legs removed by the company because she went to the bathroom too often. After she had gotten severely sick while working there, they fired her. They shut off the power to her legs, since they can control the power to the limbs they manufacture, and left her to die in a snowbank outside the building. She died in my arms when I found her later."

Avory stood up in shock and watched as Andromeda began to tremble. She sat down on the couch next to Andromeda and patted her shoulder. "I'm sorry," she mumbled.

"After Mia died," continued Andromeda, wiping the tears that began to well up in her eyes, "and after I had my hands hacked off by some sonofabitch named John M., I was given these manufactured ones by Omega."

"So those hands of yours are controlled by Omega?" asked Avory.

"No," replied Andromeda. "The man who made them for me hated the Omega Corporation as well and secretly made a set of hands that could be controlled only by me and not by the Omega power grid."

"What was his reasoning for doing that for you?" asked Avory.

"He said that he and his father, who died on the work floor there, saw that there was something special about me," answered Andromeda. "They learned of my credentials from the university that I attended abroad and wanted me to get out of that place as soon as possible. If Omega found out about my knowledge in nuclear and atomic studies, they would have forced me to work for them and the government in that department . . . otherwise, they would kill me."

"I want to tell you something," cut in Avory. "I promise that what you say will be safe with me, as long as what I tell you is safe with you."

"And me!" shouted Turd.

Avory smiled at the animal. "Yes, you too, Turd." She laughed. "Is that okay with you, Andromeda?"

"Of course," sighed Andromeda with a chuckle.

"You blew up the Omega Corporation building, didn't you?" asked Avory. "All of us at the Christmas party know you did."

Andromeda looked up stunned. "How?" she asked.

"Mark knows a lot," replied Avory. "I might as well tell you—he isn't even a human being. Mark is a vampire, and Audrey is undead as well."

Andromeda's eyes widened in disbelief at Avory.

"That whole group at the Christmas party is in on a lot of the things that go on in this town," continued Avory. "You know the band? Well, they all are supernatural beings or humans who are in on it. We know and despise the current state of our world and try to maintain a secret society to protect ourselves."

"Are you some form of supernatural being?" asked Andromeda.

"No," replied Avory. "I was a poor, starving guitar player who Mark brought into his band and home. After growing closer with him and Audrey, I became one of the human counterparts of the society."

"What does this secret society do?" Andromeda whispered.

"We manage to help our people, and the town, in any way we can without blowing our cover," replied Avory. "Mark has the ability to see and learn things going on around him while undercover, since he has the ability to change into just about any creature you can think of. He let us know about your situation once he learned of your return to our town."

"That's creepy," said Andromeda bluntly.

"It is and it isn't," cut in Avory, coming to Mark's defense. "He merely wants the best for everyone and wants to maintain as much peace as possible in town. Mark would never abuse his abilities or breach someone's privacy for his own gain or interests."

"Okay," said Andromeda, nodding in understanding. "So, what do you guys know about me, then?"

"We know you're the one who blew up the Omega building but were also the one that saved the area by eliminating the radioactive fallout," Avory answered. "We understand that you want to do everything in your ability to foil Omega's plans to rebuild as well, and we wish to help."

Andromeda stared at the blue-haired girl, her mouth open in shock. "Really?" she stammered. "You would want to help me?"

"Of course," said Avory seriously. "I came to you today, at Mark's suggestion, to ask about getting a job at Omega to see if I, an innocent human looking for employment, can get into the job fair with you, a past worker, as evidenced by your hands. If I can get into the job fair and banquet they are holding, it could possibly help you to gain access to one of the heads of Omega who would be attending. My presence would be a distraction for them so you could get in without drawing much attention to yourself."

Andromeda glanced over at Turd, and the animal slowly smiled back at her. "Okay," she said, after a pause to think. "I want to get in there and warn them privately against building again."

"We understand the power you have achieved through your invention," responded Avory, nodding. "From here on out, you do your thing. However, just let us know what we can do to help. We are here for you, Andromeda. Do you have an escape plan? Should things go south and you need to skip town, do you have a means of getting away safely?"

Andromeda looked over at Turd, then Avory, her eyes darting as a thought crossed her mind that she hadn't let out yet. "Actually," she started, "I do have an escape plan."

Turd cocked his head in question. "Really, Doc?" he asked.

Avory glanced at him, then back to Andromeda.

"Yes," Andromeda continued. "My father was an inventor. It is something that I never really talked about with anyone. He invented a flying machine, and it is held in a private hangar located on some land he purchased many years ago. He wanted to use it in case our family ever needed to get out of the country for any reason."

"That explains a lot," said Turd. "That's where you got the brains and knack for inventing things."

Andromeda blushed a little at his comment. "So anyway," she continued. "The flying machine is a lighter-than-air ship, and it can fly to higher altitudes than radar can pick up. My father would have wanted me to use it if I needed to. He showed me how to navigate it. It took him ten years to build it, and I spent quite a lot of time with him as he did so when I was in my teens."

"The society and I would be happy to help you get it ready," said Avory. "You know, if it needs any work to get it prepared for an emergency flight."

"I'll for sure let you guys be involved," said Andromeda. "I'm very thankful for the offer to help me."

"Of course," muttered Avory, finishing her cup of tea. "So . . . we will get the gang together soon to go see this airship your dad made, but first we need to get a game plan together for this coming Saturday at the job fair and banquet."

Andromeda and Avory continued to talk about what they would wear for the coming occasion and figured they would play things by ear and work off each other while at the job fair. They also figured that the best time to get the chance to meet whoever was a head of the Omega Corporation would be during the banquet. Turd was included in this operation. He was to act as an emergency distraction should anything go wrong at the banquet, since animals were not allowed, and be the eyes and ears from outside the Harris Hotel, the place that was holding the event, while Andromeda and Avory were inside.

Once they thought the game plan was in order, Avory bid Andromeda and Turd farewell. As she attempted to head out the door, Avory was met by a sharp gust of cold winter wind to her face.

"Ugh," Avory sighed, closing her eyes and exhaling long and hard. "There's snow . . . everywhere."

Andromeda quickly offered to drive Avory back into town upon learning that the girl had walked all the way to her house. Avory accepted, and the three hopped into the VW and drove off.

After leaving Avory at Mark's Bar, where she wanted to be dropped off, Andromeda drove back home. "Well, that was pretty cool," said Turd as he and Andromeda sat back down in the living room. "I'm glad that we have help now."

"Yes," said Andromeda. "I think we are definitely going to need it, now that we will be dealing with a much larger situation."

"Because blowing up a building wasn't large enough," laughed Turd.

"Exactly," snickered Andromeda. "Now let's lie low for the rest of the evening. Got a big day tomorrow."

"What's going on tomorrow?" asked the animal.

"I have to manufacture some things in the lab," replied Andromeda. "I had another idea that I think will come in handy."

"What now?" asked Turd, rolling his eyes.

"I have an idea to add to our game plan," explained Andromeda. "So we have the flying machine to use as a getaway if we need to skip the country, but we don't have the means to prevent trouble should something happen concerning the building of the new Omega plant. I have a feeling they are going to start the construction as soon as possible, and I'll be able to gather more information on that, I'm sure, at the job fair."

"What were you thinking?" asked Turd.

"I want to make some small bombs that can be detonated remotely to deter anyone attempting to build on the site or anyone raiding our home. They would be small enough, grenade sized, to scare off perpetrators, and I would fuse them with my radiation neutralizer so there wouldn't be any remaining radiation."

"You're like a superhero or something," remarked Turd. "Living up to your name of Fallout. Being in control of an actual fallout."

Andromeda smiled with a gleeful sparkle in her yellow eyes. "I guess I am," she muttered.

Andromeda and Turd spent most of the next morning in the lab, working on the small explosives that she had mentioned the evening before. She planned to plant them in certain areas of the field where the Omega site was to be rebuilt, and in emergency deterrent areas around her home should anyone try to break in in the future. She knew, without a doubt, that once things got out about what she was capable of, Omega would be hot on her trail in no time. Keeping her thoughts in preparatory mode helped Andromeda maintain a good mental state, limiting the moments that sent her into that angry form of catatonia.

Once they had completed the devices in the lab, Andromeda and Turd drove out to the Omega site. They figured that the field wouldn't be guarded anymore, given that the radiation had disappeared, and they were correct. Not only was there not a police officer in sight, but also no scientist personnel wandering around. They were able to bury the explosives rather quickly in areas Andromeda figured would be the best to deter construction vehicles before they would be able to start breaking ground.

Wiping the dirt and snow that had accumulated from all the digging she had done to place the bombs from her hands, Andromeda looked at Turd with pride. "Let's go to Mark's Bar and celebrate," she said. "I could use one of Mark's wet burritos after all that work. How about you?"

"Sounds great to me, Doc!" exclaimed Turd.

The two got into the car and sped back to town. After reaching the bar, they walked inside and were greeted by Mark at the door.

"Oh, hi, you guy," said Mark in his broken English. "You guy look hungry. You want me to make food?"

"Yes, please," answered Andromeda. Turd stood by her feet and licked his lips.

Audrey walked up to them and showed them to a table. Mark went to the back of the bar to prep the kitchen area.

"So, two wet burritos," said Audrey, writing the order down on a notepad. "Anything to drink?"

"Two ginger ales, please," replied Andromeda.

Audrey left the table to give Mark the order sheet. When she returned with the food, the two at the table fell upon the burritos with a voracious appetite. Audrey chuckled as she stood next to the bar with Mark, watching them eat.

"So, Avory went and saw them," whispered Mark into Audrey's ear. "She make plans for Saturday with them at the Omega job fair."

"I hope it goes well," mumbled Audrey. "Things are going to get pretty hairy around here soon, I feel."

"We will be okay," assured Mark. "Andromeda isn't a little bit stupid girl. Neither is Avory."

Audrey nodded in agreement, then walked back over to the table as Andromeda and Turd cleaned their plates. "Busy day?" she asked, picking up the plates from the table. "It must have been, to have appetites such as those."

"Yes," replied Andromeda. "We had a lot to do today. But we got it all done."

"Good," said Audrey with a wink.

Andromeda smiled, gathering that Audrey already knew what they had been up to that afternoon.

"Be careful on your drive home," said Mark from behind the bar. "It supposed to be bad blizzard coming again."

Andromeda thanked Mark for the heads-up and then paid for their meal. As she and Turd reached the door to walk outside, they could see a large, white cloud of snow ominously looming in the distance against the blackness of the sky. The two rushed to the car and got in.

"Mark wasn't kidding," said Andromeda nervously. "That looks like a monstrous squall coming in."

"What's a squall?" asked Turd.

"It's a type of storm that has a sudden increase in wind speed that lasts for a while," answered Andromeda, starting the Beetle. "We don't want to get blown away in the snow."

She put the car into drive and spun the tires on the ice to get onto the road as fast as possible. As they drove down the slippery street, they could feel the car begin to shake as snow-filled wind gushed over the vehicle. Visibility was growing ever poorer as Andromeda peered through the windshield, with the wipers racing back and forth.

"We'd better get inside as soon as we can," she said. "This storm is going to be a doozy."

"Can't wait to crawl into my new bed," said Turd, excitedly looking out the passenger-side window. "And listen to the storm outside."

"Me too," agreed Andromeda, quickly correcting the steering wheel as the VW swerved on the ice after a strong wind gust blew it off course. "A bed sounds really good to me right about now. Not being out driving in this shit."

The wind and snow continued to pick up speed and fall hard on the little car as Andromeda pulled it into the driveway and then the garage. She pulled the garage door down behind the Beetle, and the two raced into the house and slammed the front door behind them. The house made some creaking noises and the windows rattled as the storm raged outside. Andromeda breathed a sigh of relief, knowing that they were now safely indoors and could get ready for bed.

The bedsheets felt so comfortable as Andromeda got herself between them and lay there motionless. Turd pulled a small, folded blanket from underneath the bed and wrapped himself in it before plopping down on his new bed. The house was now completely dark. Only the sounds of the roaring blizzard outside could be heard as the two fell into a deep and peaceful sleep.

Saturday morning arrived, the day on which Andromeda was to go back into the world of Omega in the form of the job fair and banquet. When she arose from her bed, Andromeda shivered away her negative thoughts concerning what she had to try to accomplish. She was glad Avory was going to be there to help, and Turd of course, but the fears were causing her adrenaline to spike dramatically.

The job fair at the Harris Hotel was to take place between 4:00 and 6:00 p.m., and the banquet was from 6:00 to 8:00 p.m. Andromeda was counting down the hours as she made herself ready for the day. After taking a soothing bath, she dried off and retrieved her black velvet dress from the closet. She had not worn it in quite a few years, and she was glad that it still looked almost brand new.

When she looked at herself in the bathroom mirror, Andromeda admired her beautiful, youthful appearance. The years, and even the hard previous year, hadn't aged her quite as badly as she had originally thought. As she patted out the wrinkles on the waist of her dress, Andromeda's eyes locked on to her metal hands. The prostheses actually matched her dress quite nicely, in a strange villain-from-an-old-noir-film sort of way. She was truly beginning to accept her appearance more and more. She was glad for this, given that it was a slow process for her to accept the changes and that she was learning to be more comfortable in her own skin.

The morning drew to a close and the afternoon crept in. Andromeda and Turd ate a late breakfast and turned on the television to see if there were any local news updates. The only updates from the news reporter were a recap of earlier events, that the Omega Corporation was planning to rebuild early in the new year and that the job fair and banquet were to have one major member of the management board in attendance. They learned that the board member was a woman named Jess Harper, and Andromeda locked that name into her mind in preparation for later on that day.

"Jess Harper, huh," said Andromeda to Turd as they sat together on the couch. "She's the one that I need to get to today."

"Maybe you'll be able to get to her privately," muttered Turd. "But at a big event such as this, I greatly doubt it."

"I'll find a way," said Andromeda. "I have to find a way."

The doorbell rang, and Andromeda quickly stood up to answer it. It was Avory at the door, standing on the front stoop with a plethora of large snow drifts piled up behind her. The storm from the night before had left a great quantity of snowfall. Andromeda invited Avory into the house and let her warm herself up in the living room.

"The snow is probably going to limit the number of people in attendance today," said Andromeda to Avory, handing her a cup of coffee.

"For sure," mumbled Avory, taking a sip from the cup. "Hopefully Omega won't cancel the event."

"They won't," said Andromeda with a sigh. "Omega is in desperate need of people. If they want something, snow or shine, they will get it."

Avory nodded in agreement. "Yeah, I guess," she muttered, taking another sip of coffee.

"I don't know if you watched the news this morning," said Andromeda, "but it looks like the head that will be in attendance at the fair and banquet is some lady named Jess Harper."

"So, that must be the person to get to," nodded Avory.

"Looks like it," agreed Andromeda. "I'm just hoping that there will be an opportunity to talk to her in private."

"We will find a way," said Avory, reassuringly. "It may be difficult, but we will find a way nonetheless."

They sat in the living room for a while and conversed about more mundane things before three o'clock rolled around and it was time to leave for the Harris Hotel. Avory brought a three-way set of earbud communicators with her so that she, Andromeda, and Turd could be in communication with one another at the event should they get separated. Turd was to be the eyes and ears on the outside of the building, and he needed to be able to reach them. Both Avory's and Andromeda's hair was long enough to cover their ears, so concealing the communicators would not be an issue. The three climbed into the Beetle and drove off toward their destination.

The Harris Hotel was on the far west end of town. It stood roughly five miles west of Mark's Bar and General Store, at the end of the normally busy Main Street district in the heart of the town, near a wooded area composed of acres of pine trees. The hotel was one of the oldest buildings in the district, and the town had spent a great deal of money renovating it years before to make it a tourist attraction.

As Andromeda drove down Main Street, Mark's Bar and General Store came up on the right as they headed westward. The three packed into the car noticed Mark and Audrey shoveling snow from the entrance door and waved to them. Mark and Audrey smiled and waved back. Mark quickly gave them a thumbs-up. Avory, in the passenger seat, gave him a thumbs-up in response and looked over at Andromeda.

"They know," said Avory to Andromeda with a wink.

Andromeda nodded and nervously exhaled as she clutched the steering wheel. "That's good," she said. "I'm seriously hoping that this whole ordeal goes smoothly."

"Just don't worry too much," mumbled Avory. "Take it one step at a time, and try to act as natural as possible."

"Right," nodded Andromeda, her yellow eyes darting. "We are just going in to see about employment, and to make connections."

Turd, from the back seat, glanced from Andromeda to Avory then back again stiffly.

"And I'm just a dog left in the car," he said with a chuckle.

The two women giggled at his comment as the hotel came into view. Andromeda pulled the car into the large parking lot in front of the Harris and parked it in the most secluded spot available. She didn't want the foot traffic of prospective employees near the vehicle to be too great, although she figured that in the bustle of the crowds, it would go mostly unnoticed. As Andromeda and Avory got out of the vehicle, they noticed that there was a large number of cars in the parking lot.

"That's a good sign," said Andromeda. She smiled at Avory. "A very good sign."

Avory quietly grabbed Andromeda by the arm as they walked and pointed to a fairly large group of people walking across the lot to the Harris. Andromeda gasped at the sight. The group was composed of prosthesis-laden individuals. Their faces were blank and tired looking, and their robotic limbs appeared to move on their own toward the front of the hotel.

"They're being controlled by Omega," whispered Andromeda to a quizzical Avory.

"Maybe you should pretend they are controlling you too," whispered Avory.

"Good idea," agreed Andromeda, stiffening her hands and making them appear as if they were more robotic, not moving as naturally as she was now able to.

They walked into the front entrance of the hotel and were greeted by a stone-faced gentleman who asked them to sign a guest registry. Avory signed her name, but Andromeda signed hers as Dr. Andromeda Fallout.

*Allison Finkle is dead*, thought Andromeda to herself. *You're Dr. Andromeda Fallout now . . . remember that.*

The main hall of the job fair was packed with people, some of whom had prosthetic limbs and some of whom were young and bright eyed. There were vibes of both reluctance and excitement in the air. Andromeda glanced sadly at the young people standing near the tables as they chatted with the Omega interviewers with their fake smiles. Her heart began to melt as she watched the young and innocent eyes of the prospective employees as they tried their best to impress this company with their interviewing skills.

"I was like that," muttered Andromeda to Avory as her eyes began to burn with sadness and rage.

Avory placed her hand on Andromeda's arm and squeezed. "Keep it together," she whispered, her eyes beginning to fill with concern. "It'll be okay."

"Whatever you do," whispered Andromeda. "Do *not* sign any paperwork they may or may not offer you. They are sneaky bastards, and you don't want to get stuck in any way with them legally."

"What about the registry we signed?" questioned Avory.

"It was just a normal book register," answered Andromeda. "I looked it over well. It was just for their past employee memory bank.

Neither of us put in job numbers, since we don't have one, and neither of us have names in their system."

Avory nodded and sighed in relief.

The two girls walked up to a table, and each was questioned by a separate interviewer, but they were able to stand there and be interviewed side by side. Avory played the wide-eyed innocent; Andromeda was surprised the girl could actually snap out of her serious and often depressed demeanor so quickly. The Omega interviewer questioned Andromeda's past employment history upon looking at her hands. Andromeda managed to say that she had received the appliances from a third party, and the interviewer actually believed her. She was very relieved that that was all it took to convince the interviewer of the reason for the metal appendages that hung at her sides.

The interviewers handed each woman a pamphlet containing information on the next steps for employment, and they were not required to sign anything. Andromeda carefully looked at the pamphlet after they left the table.

She noticed on the last page that a flat metal microchip was attached at the bottom.

"When you have the opportunity to do so," whispered Andromeda into Avory's ear, pointing a finger at the metal chip, "throw your pamphlet away. As soon as possible."

Avory's mouth dropped open as she opened her pamphlet to the last page, spotted the chip, and nodded in agreement.

"I told you," continued Andromeda. "They're sneaky bastards. It's no doubt collecting GPS whereabouts or some other form of information."

After the two managed to dispose of the pamphlets in the bathroom, they walked back out to the main hall. Someone bumped into Andromeda. She looked over to see who it was, and a lady with a short haircut and wearing a business suit met her eyes.

"Pardon me," said the lady cordially. "I didn't mean to run into you."

Andromeda looked down at the woman. "It's okay," she said politely while extending her hand. "I'm Dr. Andromeda Fallout. What's your name?"

The lady extended her arm and received Andromeda's handshake. "I'm Jess Harper," she replied in a tone loaded with arrogance. "I'm one of the chief executive officers of the Omega Corporation. May I ask in what field is your doctorate? Miss Fallout?"

Avory quickly glanced up at Andromeda, while Andromeda tried to maintain the rush of adrenaline she felt.

"I have a doctorate in nuclear and atomic radiation studies. It is a pleasure to make your acquaintance," replied Andromeda, forcing a smile to her lips. "I heard about you on the local news."

"Yes," continued Jess. "I oversee all of the management concerning the Omega Corporation locations, and their construction as well."

"Is that why you are here today?" Avory asked Harper.

"Yes," she replied. "I'm here to look over the plans and communicate with our partners, since we plan to rebuild here in your town after the new year."

Andromeda stared down, towering over Jess, with a flame burning in each of her yellow irises. "That will be exciting," she murmured. "I'm glad that the fallout caused by the disaster disappeared so quickly."

Jess looked up into Andromeda's stare. Questions and suspicion filled her eyes. "Me too," she agreed. "Never in the history of modern science has such a phenomenon occurred."

"Yes . . . very interesting," muttered Andromeda.

Avory felt a surge of anticipation as she glanced between the towering Andromeda and the upward-staring Jess. She entertained the thought that she was watching a Western standoff, like in a movie she recalled with Alan

Ladd and Jack Palance, waiting to see who was going to skin their smoke wagon first. She tried to shrug off the thought.

"I was wondering," said Jess, breaking the silence, "if you would be interested in having a meeting with me, Miss Andromeda, at some point during the banquet."

"What for?" asked Andromeda sternly.

Avory's lip quivered as she looked upon the situation.

"Oh, no real reason," replied Jess. "I just want to talk with you. Being a doctor and all of nuclear studies, I am very interested in having a little one-on-one conversation with you. Would that be all right?"

Andromeda couldn't believe how easily all these opportunities were falling into place concerning her and Avory's mission. "That would be quite all right," she smiled, shaking the fire from her eyes and replacing it with a kind gleam.

Jess shook Andromeda's hand again in a professional manner and made an appointment for them to meet her at her temporary office, which was on an upper floor in the hotel, during the latter portion of the banquet. After everything was set in stone, Andromeda and Avory walked away. A cold and suspicious look crossed Jess's face as she turned and disappeared into the crowd of people around the room.

The job fair drew to a close and the banquet began. Andromeda and Avory sat down at a table in the corner of the room, alone, and tapped in a call on their communicator earbuds.

"Hello, Turd?" said Andromeda as quietly as possible. "Are the communicators working?"

"Loud and clear, Doc," responded Turd.

"Is mine working too, Turd?" asked Avory.

"Yours is as well," replied the dog.

"We are almost done with the event, Turd," explained Andromeda. "Are you staying warm in the car?"

"Yeah," replied the animal. "Good thing we brought a blanket and I have my Christmas sweater. Is everything going okay?"

"Sure is," said Andromeda. "I have a meeting with a head in about fifteen minutes."

"Yes, everything fell right into her lap," chimed in Avory.

Andromeda smiled at Avory's comment. "Be ready, Turd," continued Andromeda nervously. "Things could get ugly. Keep an eye out for any police, should they arrive, and let us know, so Avory will be down and ready to leave and get you both out of here if I can't manage to get away."

"Please get away, Doc," whimpered Turd. "I don't want to lose you."

Andromeda breathed in deep. "I'll do my best," she stammered.

The banquet dragged on for what seemed like hours as Andromeda and Avory picked at the food on their plates. Andromeda looked up at the clock and figured it was about time for her to make the journey upstairs to Jess Harper's office.

"Okay," she said to Avory while Turd listened in on the communicator. "I'm going in."

Andromeda cautiously arose from her seat at the table. Avory clutched her hand and held it in reassurance. Andromeda nodded in understanding with a caring smile. She walked from the room in which the banquet was being held and out into a hallway that contained the elevator. Andromeda pressed the up button, and the elevator door opened. She entered the elevator and turned to see Avory standing in the hall looking at her. They exchanged nods as the doors closed between them.

Andromeda stood in front of the closed elevator doors with great anticipation. She tried to maintain her composure through some breathing exercises. The elevator buttons indicating the floors lit up, moving closer and closer to the floor where she needed to get off. She clenched her metal fists tightly for a moment, then released them to straighten her dress and hair in the mirror in the elevator. As she looked at her reflection, Andromeda felt a flood of emotions come over her. They stemmed from memories that crashed into her mind like great flashes of lightning, flashes that hit and burned random spots in the landscape that was her brain.

*Your eyes told me . . . Everyone's eyes are dead or blank. You know what I mean? The life is gone from them. Once I saw yours, I knew you were special . . .* Mia's words rang in her ears as if her friend was still there, standing next to her, not dead. Andromeda looked at her glowing yellow irises, peering into them as if searching for that special something Mia must have seen in them a long time ago. Was it still there?

Images of Olin as he lay dying on the floor in the Omega plant snapped into her mind, and the words of his son, the man who made her hand prostheses, sounded once again: *You didn't deserve to have your hands removed . . . This is my payback to you for being kind to my father when he needed it most . . .*

Andromeda tried to shake these thoughts, even though she knew they were a driving force in her soul. They would never disappear completely from her. They would continue on until her life was complete.

The elevator doors opened. Andromeda stood erect as the doors revealed her tall, stubborn, and cold demeanor before she walked out into the hallway that met her. She strode slowly, yet with a slight hop in her step, as her shiny-black metallic hands glistened in the dim lights of the hall. Her eyes peered up with a fierce determination from beneath the bangs that swept across her forehead. She reached the door to Jess's office, which had "Jess Harper" emblazoned on a label on the wood, and cautiously knocked.

"Come in," came a voice from within.

Andromeda opened the door carefully. The room was dark, with only one light illuminating a corner that revealed Jess sitting at a desk.

"Hello again, Miss Fallout," said Jess Harper from behind the desk, her face partially lit by the lamp.

"Hello, Miss Harper," answered Andromeda as she cautiously entered the room.

"Please," continued Jess. "Have a seat."

"I'll stand," said Andromeda coldly.

"Suit yourself," answered Jess, a sly grin crossing her lips. "So let's cut to the chase here, Miss Fallout . . ."

"Call me Andromeda," interrupted Andromeda.

"Okay," stammered Jess. "Let's cut to the chase, Andromeda."

"I'm all about cutting through the bullshit, Miss Harper," said Andromeda, staring deep into Jess's somewhat nervous gaze.

"Call me Jess," quipped the woman. "Now . . . it has come to our attention that someone has created a means of neutralizing radiation in vast quantities, in a short amount of time."

"I wonder who that could be?" asked Andromeda, with great sarcasm in her voice.

"We both know it was you," whispered Jess.

Andromeda walked up to the desk and placed her hand on it with a soft metal clunk. "What makes you say that?" she asked.

"They never found the body of a certain tall, blond employee who had hand prostheses after the explosion," replied Jess, her voice growing angrier and angrier. "And whatever remained of the Omega employee forms in our computer system, all points to a certain Allison Finkle as the major culprit of that disaster."

Andromeda's face remained stern and unmoving as she stared bullets into the woman behind the desk.

"We don't have any evidence of this," continued Jess. "But personally? I feel that it was *you*, Miss Allison Finkle."

"You know what else you may feel?" asked Andromeda, beginning to smile.

"No," replied Jess, annoyed.

Andromeda slammed her hands down onto the desk and, in an instant, flipped it over to the side of the room. Jess gasped and stood up. Before Jess could come to terms with what had just happened, Andromeda grabbed her by the lapels and pinned her up against the wall.

"My name is Andromeda Fallout, bitch!" she hissed through her teeth, glaring death into Jess's eyes. "Allison Finkle is dead! *Never*, I repeat, *never* call me by that name again!"

Jess stared wide-eyed and shaking at the fierce predator that had her pinned up against the wall.

"And if you think you'll be able to get *me* to work for Omega again," continued Andromeda, "you have another thing coming! The company has another thing coming! Do you understand?"

"You'll have no choice," said Jess with a smirk, although choking on her words in Andromeda's grip. "With knowledge like yours, you won't be able to keep your secrets hidden from us, or the government, forever."

"I hold the only key to this discovery," growled Andromeda. "And I work for no one except myself and my beliefs. It is only for those who need it, deserve it, and for the benefit of the human race. Not for a piece-of-shit corporation like Omega, or the bastards who run it. I will die before I turn *any* of it over to you."

"You're going to die anyway," gasped Jess under the weight of Andromeda's fingers. "Just try and hide. We will find you either way."

Andromeda clenched her hands tighter around Jess's throat. "No, you won't," she hissed, gritting her teeth, her eyes filled with fiery anger. "You decide to build another Omega plant in my town? Good luck. It won't happen. You try to start a war with me? Good luck. You won't win."

Jess spat in her face in defiance and chuckled.

Andromeda thrust Jess across the room. Jess's body slammed into a wall and came crashing down onto a filing cabinet, then onto the floor. Jess attempted to get up but instead lay shaking and coughing. Andromeda walked over and stood over her body.

"I came to warn you," said Andromeda sternly. "Not to threaten you, but to warn you against coming back to find me. Also to warn you about building again, or forcing the Omega Corporation and its practices back onto my town and its people."

"Go to hell," stammered Jess.

"Already been there and back," retorted Andromeda. "I'm here to help innocent people from persecution by people like yourself. Now go eat dirt, and I hope I never have to see your ugly mug again. If I do? You *will* die."

Andromeda turned and left Jess lying on the floor in shock. She calmly yet briskly walked back down the hall and into the elevator. She began to hyperventilate as her adrenaline levels began to crash and her anger began to ebb.

"Come on, come on," growled Andromeda at the elevator's floor indicator as it worked its way downward. "Please hurry . . ."

The elevator reached the main floor and the doors opened. Andromeda was met by the wide-eyed expression of Avory, standing just outside the doors.

"We have to get out of here," muttered Andromeda urgently.

"I overheard the whole thing on the communicator," said Avory as she powerwalked next to Andromeda toward the hotel entrance. "You gave Jess Harper a run for her money with that little spat. Things are definitely going to get hairy around here now."

Andromeda sighed and closed her eyes as she pushed the entrance door open, letting Avory speed past her. They continued to walk as fast as possible across the parking lot to the car, where Turd sat staring intently out the window. Avory and Andromeda quickly opened the car doors and climbed in.

"Step on it," ordered Avory.

Andromeda speedily but carefully maneuvered the Beetle around the cars that packed the parking lot and onto the main road.

"It might be a good idea for me to call Mark and Audrey when we get back to your house," said Avory. "At least give them the rundown of what happened and see what they can do to help."

"Okay." Andromeda nodded, her face twitching with anxiety.

"Good idea," agreed Turd.

Andromeda began to shake as she drove.

"Just calm down," whispered Avory, laying a hand on Andromeda's shoulder. "Just breathe. You're doing great. Those mother-monkeys didn't know what they were up against until this evening."

"Totally!" exclaimed Turd reassuringly. "Dr. Andromeda Fallout strikes again!"

Andromeda slowly smiled and let a tiny giggle rise from her throat. "I'll be the alpha, the beginning, to Omega's omega," she chuckled.

Avory and Turd began to laugh at Andromeda's witty remark.

Once Andromeda got the Beetle safely parked in the garage and the door shut behind it, she and the other two began to hear the sounds of sirens in the distance. They raced into the house and locked the door behind them. They peered through a curtain over the front window and watched as several police cruisers began to speed past the house and down the street into town.

"They were alerted," murmured Avory.

Andromeda stood back from the window and wiped the nervous perspiration from her forehead. "They're going to know where I live," she uttered. "Jess Harper will tell all, since she concluded that I was Allison Finkle. Omega probably has my address on file somewhere. If it was contained in a databank, not just in a paper file."

"Let's hope they don't," said Avory. "There still might be the chance that it was destroyed in the explosion."

"Truth," sighed Andromeda. "I can only hope. Otherwise, I will have to use the emergency explosive field I set as protection around the house. I don't want to have to use it yet, since I haven't been able to make it to the airship and make sure that it's in working order first."

Avory turned from the window and toward Andromeda. "When I call Mark and Audrey here shortly, I'll inform them about the airship so they can get out there tomorrow morning to look it over with us . . . If there isn't a ton of police action out on the streets, of course."

Andromeda smiled with relief. "That would be wonderful," she said. "Thank you!"

Avory went over to the phone that was hanging on the wall in the kitchen and made the call. After a quick conversation, she returned to the living room. Andromeda and Turd sat waiting in anticipation of Avory's return.

"All set," said Avory. "Mark, Audrey, Phineas, Betty, and myself will be at your house early tomorrow morning. Should traffic permit, and if the police clear the area, we should be out to the airship and ready to work in no time."

"Are you just going to stay here for the night?" asked Andromeda. "You're more than welcome to stay."

"Thank you," replied Avory. "That would be most convenient, you see."

"I do see," chuckled Andromeda at Avory.

"By the way," started Avory. "What are the explosive field protection things you mentioned earlier? The ones around the house."

"They are remote-controlled detonation mines to deter anyone trying to raid the house," Andromeda explained. "I have also placed several in the field where the Omega Corporation wants to rebuild. They are nuclear in function and quite destructive. However, I have placed my radiation neutralizer invention in them, so the detonations won't leave any traces of dangerous radiation."

"If you end up leaving town," said Avory, "you won't be able to prevent them from rebuilding. Wouldn't it have been better to just leave the fallout in the area after you detonate them? It would prevent Omega from being able to rebuild there."

"Already thought of that," replied Andromeda.

"You have?" asked Turd.

"Yes," answered Andromeda. "The radiation-neutralizer function within the explosives can be turned on or off prior to or after detonation. So if I wanted to create a safer means for the area, I could. But also, I can create a danger zone if need be."

"You're in control, Doc," murmured Turd, grinning.

"You definitely live up to your name," said Avory admiringly.

Andromeda blushed at their comments. "Aw, shucks," she said. "Now, enough of this chitchat. Let's make some actual dinner and get some rest. The food at that banquet was absolutely disgusting. We need some real food."

"Agreed," mumbled Avory. "Leave it to Omega to have cardboard for fancy banquet food. Stinking cheapskates."

Andromeda laughed to learn they were both thinking the same thing about it at the banquet, even though nothing was said. They went into the kitchen to prepare a meal for themselves. The dinner consisted of chicken with lemon pepper seasoning and a bottle of sparkling cider.

Upon taking a sip of the cider, Avory looked up at Andromeda and Turd and smiled in surprise. "You know what?" she asked the others.

"What?" they asked in unison.

"It's just about midnight," Avory replied. "You know what that means?"

"It's getting late," said Andromeda.

"True," continued Avory. "But you know what else?"

Turd and Andromeda looked at her questioningly.

"Happy New Year," muttered Avory, rolling her eyes.

Andromeda began to chuckle as a wide smile grew on her face. "Happy New Year, everyone," she said, raising her glass to toast the others. They all did so, and clinked their glasses.

The next morning arrived, and Turd was the first to wake up. As he stretched his limbs and got up, he poked his head around the foot of the bed to check and see if Andromeda was awake. All he could see was her arm as it dangled off the side of the bed, and he could hear the sounds of her snoring. Turd figured he wouldn't wake her quite yet but wanted to check on the rest of the house. He quietly moved his paws across the cold floor as he went into the living room, where Avory lay passed out on the couch. When he saw the front door, the sudden urge to use the bathroom hit him. Turd tried to hold in a whimper so as to not wake Avory.

"You have to take a piss or something?" came Avory's monotone voice from the couch.

"Please?" whimpered Turd.

With a deep sigh and a grunt, Avory rose from the couch and half stumbled to the door as she tried to regain her bearings after sleep. She opened the door and let the dog out. After Turd had finished his business, Avory let him back inside. Turd thanked her for helping him as she sat on the couch trying to wake up.

"I need coffee or something," Avory mumbled.

"Me too," came a voice from behind them as Andromeda appeared, the tall woman looking very disheveled. Turd tried to hold in a laugh upon seeing her.

"Looks like you slept hard," said Avory, rubbing her eyes.

Andromeda nodded as she stiffly moved from the living room to the kitchen to turn on the coffee pot. Laying her head on the kitchen counter, Andromeda waited for the coffee to be ready. After the machine indicated the coffee was done, she poured a cup for herself and Avory. She brought the steaming cups into the living room and handed one to her guest.

"Today is the day, huh?" Turd asked the two women as they sat hunched over on the couch. "To go to see the airship?"

"Yes, sir," replied Andromeda as she cracked her stiff neck. She gasped.

Turd and Avory looked over at her in concern.

"That was needed," Andromeda whispered, smiling contentedly.

"Provided you don't break your neck beforehand," Avory said jokingly, "when do you think would be a good time to get the group here and head over to the airship?"

"Pretty soon," answered Andromeda, taking a sip of her coffee. "Just have to wake up and get dressed. Everything we would need to do any repairs is in the hangar where the airship is sitting. So, all we need to bring are ourselves."

"That's good," said Avory, finishing her coffee. "Hopefully we can manage to get over to the location without any authorities' suspicious eyes watching us. Especially after yesterday."

Andromeda nodded in agreement. "Well," she said with a sigh, "I'm going to get dressed and get this day started."

"I'll give Mark a call right now," said Avory, moving from the couch and into the kitchen to dial the phone.

When Andromeda returned from the bathroom after getting ready for the day, she asked Avory what the status was with the others and when they were to arrive. Avory told her that Mark, Audrey, Betty, and Phineas planned to come over as soon as possible but that they were taking a short drive first to scope out the roads to see the status of any police activity in the area.

When the others finally did arrive, they were welcomed into Andromeda's home. "There wasn't much police activity at all out there," said Audrey. "We should be good to go. Although I'm surprised that there wasn't."

Andromeda breathed in nervously. "Me too," she said. "We will need to act fast. Did any of you guys learn anything on the news at all? We didn't get the chance to catch the morning news bulletin."

"Yeah," answered Mark. "They mention that they want to do public search for someone who cause problem at the banquet. But nothing more."

"No one has been to my house yet," said Andromeda. "So, I guess that's a good thing. However, Jess Harper seemed to be someone that had a keen eye on things that had been going on behind the scenes with Omega, and after yesterday, with how my meeting with her went, I wouldn't put it past her if she had something in the works right now."

"Let's consider ourselves lucky that the streets are quiet this morning," said Audrey. "Now, how far do we have to drive to get to this airship?"

"The hangar is located about fifteen minutes east of town," replied Andromeda. "The snow from the last blizzard we had will probably make the road leading to it a bit precarious, with possible drifting, but it's a pretty straightforward drive otherwise. It's on Old Mill Road."

"Let's get moving then!" exclaimed Betty in her ever-booming voice.

The group exited Andromeda's house. Andromeda, Turd, and Avory climbed into the VW Beetle, while the others piled into Mark's black 1978 Lincoln Mark V. After starting the engines, the Beetle's buzzing hum and the Lincoln's burbly rumble filled the air as the two vehicles pulled out onto the street and toward Old Mill Road. The weather was clear, and the sun shone brightly on the fields surrounding the country road. The clarity of the weather was ideal for the groups in the cars, the VW leading and the Lincoln following close behind, in that it gave everyone a great view of the area to keep an eye out for police monitoring.

They had driven most of the way to their destination when, about five minutes out, a police cruiser pulled out behind Mark's Lincoln. "Oh, shit!" exclaimed Andromeda, looking in the rearview mirror. "There's company behind us!"

The three in the Beetle looked behind them and watched as Mark pulled his car off to the side of the road, with the police car flashing its lights behind him. "It'll be okay," mumbled Avory. "Mark will come up with something."

Mark sat behind the wheel of the Lincoln and sighed. "This suck little bit," he said to Audrey, who was sitting in the passenger seat. Betty sat panting in the back seat with Phineas.

"We are such toast," whispered Betty, hyperventilating. "We are such burnt toast."

"Relax, Betty," murmured Audrey. "We are simply out for a drive. That is all they need to know. So keep your mouth shut, and Mark will handle this."

The police officer walked up to Mark's window and tapped on it. Mark politely rolled it down. "Is there problem, officer?" he asked.

"We are monitoring the area today," replied the officer. "We are looking for a tall blond woman. Have you seen a tall blond woman lately?"

"No, wish," said Mark, glancing over at Audrey in a joking manner. Audrey rolled her eyes at his remark.

"Thank you, sir," said the officer at the window. "Have a nice day."

The officer walked back to his cruiser, while the group in Mark's car breathed a sigh of relief.

"That was easy," said Phineas.

"Yes, that was a close call," said Audrey while Mark put the car into drive and pulled forward. "I'm glad he pulled over our car, not Andromeda's."

Back in the VW, Andromeda kept the car moving, but slowly, as Mark eventually caught back up to her in his car.

"I'm glad they're back on the road," Andromeda said. "We're almost there."

The two cars continued down Old Mill Road until a large aircraft hangar came into view. The hangar sat in the middle of a large open field covered in snow. The field itself was surrounded by several miles of trees, which kept the view of the hangar hidden from the surrounding areas. As the cars came to a stop just outside the hangar's main door, the two groups quickly got out of them and followed Andromeda to the entrance. When she opened the door, everyone tiptoed into the hangar and saw its ceiling towering above them.

It was very dark inside, illuminated only by sunlight coming through the small rectangular windows near the roof. Sunbeams cast small rays of light into the darkness, exposing the amazing invention that stood towering in the center of the floor. A long, rigid gondola cabin with bubble-like windows sat latched to the top of a large, heavy, rolling cart. An enormous balloon was attached to the top of the gondola. The balloon, or gas chamber, stood sixty-four feet tall, one hundred and ninety-seven feet long, and fifty-five feet wide. The gondola could hold just over twenty passengers, including the pilot.

The exterior of the entire structure had a unique appearance. The exterior of the gondola had a shiny and streamlined coat of metal panels, like the retro-futuristic architecture of the 1950s. The balloon itself came to a sharp point in the front and a rounded point in the back and was a gray metallic color. Several large metal spikes lined the center of the balloon and stretched over the top, from the front to the back, like a single-file parade of shark fins. Four turbo-propeller air-cooled gasoline engines sat attached to each side of the gondola, one on each quarter, capable of producing a total of eight hundred horsepower. The craft was built to achieve speeds exceeding 128.75 kilometers per hour, or eighty miles per hour. The group stood in awe of the massive structure that stood before them.

"Oh wow, cool," muttered Mark, his mouth wide open.

"I should say," agreed Audrey.

"That there thing," said Betty, "is a monster."

Andromeda walked forward from the group to the airship and placed her hand gently on the side of the gondola. "My father worked hard on this," she said to the group. "He never got the chance to take a trip in it before he died, and he would be so happy if we could get his creation off the ground."

"I'm sure he would be proud," said Turd, "for it to help his daughter, who obviously has his knack for inventing things."

Andromeda smiled at the dog, then quickly turned her head back to the ship. Her lip quivered as emotions began to well up inside. "Yes," she whimpered, fighting the tears in her eyes. "I can only hope that he would be proud."

"Well," mumbled Avory, suddenly breaking the group's silence. "Let's get this thing ready or something. It won't fly itself, you see."

Andromeda nodded and smiled as the group started the work needed on the airship. With Andromeda's guidance, the group split up into different areas on the craft to make adjustments and repairs. Mark and Audrey took on the responsibility of tightening down structural components between the gondola and the balloon. Phineas and Betty performed the repairs that required welding on the gondola's main frame. Andromeda and Turd took on the responsibility of fixing and adjusting the cockpit instruments, adding some more recent radar equipment than what her father had originally placed in the craft to ensure that everything was up to date.

Andromeda decided to add some firepower to the airship in case they needed it in the future. She designed and built a system of explosives that could be dropped from the ship, similar to what she had invented and placed around her home and at the Omega site. With some help from Mark and his ability to retrieve things proficiently and secretly, four F-15E twenty-millimeter Gatling gun systems were placed outside the gondola, two facing the front and two facing the back. The guns were capable of being fired by the pilot and copilot from inside the cockpit. The airship was now ready for almost anything that should come up against her in the skies.

"What happens if someone shoots at the blimp?" Turd asked Andromeda.

"What do you mean?" replied Andromeda. "Nothing much, I don't think."

"Won't it pop like a balloon?" continued Turd. "Sending us into a flying spiral, and making us one big supersonic fart noise in the sky?"

"An airship isn't like a rubber balloon, Turd," explained Andromeda. "It won't go shooting about when the air is ejected from it. If a bullet were to hit the canvas part of the ship, it'd rip a hole, and some helium, the gas that makes us float, would leak out if it tore into a gas chamber inside. We would have to repair that as soon as we could land. But at the optimal altitude of ten thousand feet, at which we will be, the internal pressure of the helium is almost the same as the air density outside the ship. So even if we were to be hit by a lot of bullets, the helium would eject rather slowly. Let's just hope and pray we don't have to land before we reach our destination."

"What's going to be our destination?" asked Turd.

"An island," replied Andromeda. "There is an uncharted island that my father knew of. He wanted to fly this craft there someday, but he was never able to. He left a map of the course in the cockpit, and I made sure it's still there."

Turd smiled and barked in excitement. "Dr. Andromeda Fallout and her faithful companion Turd take to the skies for a high-flying adventure to an uncharted island!" he boomed in a tone like that of an old movie trailer announcer.

Andromeda smiled at the animal and went back to her work.

Now that the airship was complete and ready for flight, the group drove back to Andromeda's home for dinner. They were all very satisfied with the work they had accomplished.

"Thank you so much," smiled Andromeda to the others as they sat together in the living room with their meals. "Turd and I are much appreciative."

"We got you," said Audrey. "So, now that the balloon is armed and ready for escaping, what are your next steps?"

Andromeda thought for a moment. "I think I should let the town know about the explosives I placed at the Omega site," she said, "and see whether or not they want me to leave the area contaminated before I go."

"What was the reasoning again?" asked Betty. "For using the explosives?"

"To prevent Omega from building there again," replied Andromeda. "They didn't plan on rebuilding here in town until they discovered that the fallout levels were depleted. If I end up leaving you all, I don't want Omega to move back in and start to run things."

Betty nodded in understanding. "Yeah, that seems like a good idea," she said. "Let the town be and not get overrun by the corporation again."

"All they want is power," mumbled Andromeda. "They have such a strong pull with the government that they eventually could just turn small towns like ours into corporate entities."

"Pretty disgusting ones at that," sighed Avory.

Mark leaned back in the chair he was sitting in. "Don't worry about it," he said. "Don't worry about talking to town people. I do it for you."

"I feel like I should, though," said Andromeda. "It's my duty, since I'm the one using science and my inventions to affect the area in which they all live."

"But Omega will be hot on your trail," said Mark. "I make sure they understand."

"He will," agreed Audrey.

Andromeda sighed and looked at her plate of food as Turd nudged his head up against her leg. "You have to trust them," he whispered. "We don't know how much time we will have to stay here before Omega comes knocking on your door."

At that moment, someone knocked on the front door. Everyone in the room looked up fast, glancing from the door to each other.

"You have got to be kidding me," growled Andromeda under her breath.

"Be careful," whispered Mark seriously. "Just carefully answer door, and we will have your back."

"But . . ." stammered Andromeda fearfully.

"No buts," retorted Mark. "Go answer door."

Andromeda stood up slowly from the couch she was sitting on. She glanced at Turd and winked at him. Turd nodded and quickly ran to the bedroom. The others looked at the dog somewhat confusedly but remained quiet in their seats. Andromeda slowly and, as nonchalantly as possible, opened the front door. She gulped wide-eyed at the sight that met her eyes on the front stoop outside. It was Jess Harper, with two burly men standing behind her. Jess glared at Andromeda as a sly smile crossed her lips.

"Hello, Miss Fallout," Jess said coldly. "We knew it wouldn't be long before we found you."

"Am I that hard to find?" asked Andromeda sarcastically.

Jess growled with impatience and waved the two men forward. "Arrest her," she said.

"I'm not going anywhere," said Andromeda. "If you take one more step, you will die."

The two men backed up fearfully, while Jess seemed perplexed. As they stood there for a moment, two more people wearing suits and Omega badges appeared on the front lawn.

Andromeda stared bullets into Jess's eyes. "Tell them not to take one more step," she ordered, "or they will die as well."

Turd tiptoed into the living room from the bedroom, carrying a small metal box in his mouth. Avory bent down beside him as the others cautiously watched the events taking place at the front door.

"What's this?" Avory quietly asked Turd, taking the metal box out of his mouth.

"It's the detonator for Doc's explosive devices," whispered Turd. "She hid it in the bedroom and let only me know where it was located."

Avory bit her lip anxiously as she observed the metal box and noticed a small red button on it. She looked back up at Turd, and then to the front door.

"You're full of shit," hissed Jess at Andromeda. She began to take a step closer to the door.

Andromeda's eyes widened with rage. She noticed that the two Omega people on the lawn had begun to walk forward, ignoring her warning. "I warned you," she said. "You leave me no choice."

With that, Andromeda turned her head toward Turd in the room behind her and winked. Turd looked at Avory, who nodded and pressed the red button on the detonator. The blackness of night suddenly flashed with a bright light as the two people on the lawn disappeared in the midst of a blast from the ground beneath them. Their bloody remains splattered on the front of the house and the three people standing on the stoop as Andromeda shielded her face and slammed the door shut.

"It's time!" exclaimed Andromeda to the group, which stood stunned in the living room. "Time to get a move on!"

The front door crashed open as Jess and the two men came storming in, covered in the blood and pieces of flesh of the two victims outside.

"Kill her!" screamed Jess to the two men. "Kill Allison Finkle!"

Andromeda snarled upon hearing that name again, remembering what she had said to Jess in her office that day. She punched Jess in the mouth. Jess reeled back against the wall as the two men grabbed Andromeda by the wrists. Mark and Audrey suddenly broke the law of physics and went scrambling up the wall and onto the ceiling above the two men, like a couple of spiders. Turd watched in awe at this turn of events.

"They're not human. She's undead, and he's some kind of vampire," mumbled Avory to Turd. "Let's go help them, I guess."

Turd remained puzzled and shocked as Avory and Betty ran over to the men and grabbed each one by an arm, struggling with them. Audrey and Mark leapt down from the ceiling, landing on the two men's heads. Phineas the cat, who had remained mostly silent throughout this ordeal, leapt onto Jess's face and began to claw away at it. Jess struggled for a moment with the animal, managing to throw him off and into a wall. Phineas wearily shook his head as he struggled to get back onto his four paws after the blow.

Andromeda freed her hands from the two men's grasp, while Avory and Betty continued to hold on to the men almost helplessly, and raised her fist to knock them out. Before she could do so, Jess came at Andromeda from behind and wrapped her arms around Andromeda's throat. Andromeda gasped for air and began to stumble backward as Jess remained clinging to her from behind like a backpack.

Mark and Audrey rushed up to the two men and each grabbed one of the burly figures by the top of the head. They slammed the two men's skulls into one another, sending their large bodies to the floor with a loud thud. After looking down at the unconscious perpetrators,

Mark, Audrey, Avory, and Betty looked over at Andromeda as she stumbled backward into the kitchen with Jess on her back. They rushed to help her just as Andromeda fell onto her back and pinned Jess under her. Jess gasped in pain as the six-foot-six human being lay on top of her small body. She was choking for air.

Turd raced to Andromeda's side as the others quickly helped her to her feet, leaving Jess on the ground, wheezing. "The other detonator," panted Andromeda. "Turd, get the other detonator for the Omega site . . . before we get out of here!"

The others watched as the dog ran from the room to retrieve the detonator, then looked at Andromeda as she struggled to regain her bearings.

"I go start car," said Mark. "Need to make clean getaway."

As Mark ran out the front door, he looked around to make sure that the coast was clear. There wasn't a police officer in sight yet, but he figured they would be coming soon if they had heard the explosion that had taken place a short while before. He hopped into his Lincoln and started the engine just as the others began to exit the house and rush toward the vehicle. Andromeda and Turd were the first to get into the back seat of the Lincoln, while the others crammed themselves into the rest of the car's space as quickly as possible.

"I've got the detonator," said Andromeda to Mark as he started pulling the car out of the driveway and onto the street. "Do you think that the area will be clear for me to fire off the explosion on the Omega site?"

"You should be good to go," replied Mark. "Do it quick, we got company."

They looked out the car windows and watched as Jess appeared from inside the house with her two guards. Andromeda pressed the detonator button, and a great white light appeared in the distance behind them. Jess and the two men stood dumbfounded at the sight that met their eyes.

"She did it!" Jess screamed. "That bitch did it! We are doomed! Omega will never be rebuilt in this area without her help! Don't let her get away!"

The three climbed into the sedan in which they had arrived and sped off after the Lincoln.

"Hey," said Avory. She sat squished between Betty and the back door. "They're after us. They are catching up fast!"

Andromeda nervously looked behind her and out the back window as the other car's lights came into view. Mark slammed the pedal to the floor, sending the Lincoln skidding onto the country road toward the airship hangar.

"What do we do if they arrive at the hangar when we do?" asked Turd.

"Kill them," murmured Mark, somewhat sadly.

Andromeda stared out the windshield with tears welling up in her eyes. Turd noticed this and patted her hand with his paw in reassurance. "It'll be all right," he said. "This will all be over soon, Doc. We will be able to start afresh after tonight."

The Lincoln came roaring into the lot in front of the airship hangar and came to a sliding halt on the gravel driveway. Everyone climbed out of the car quickly as Jess and the two men arrived in their vehicle. Avory, Betty, and Phineas ran over to the large door of the hangar and began to open it with the electronic button on the wall beside it. Andromeda, Mark, and Audrey looked fearfully at the car with Jess and the two men in it. Turd raced from the Lincoln, through the opening hangar doorway, and stopped next to the airship to wait for Andromeda.

Jess and the two men got out of their car and stormed toward the group standing by the Lincoln. Andromeda glanced over at Mark and Audrey, whose faces were lit up by the headlights of the other car. Their breath came out in clouds as they nervously waited for what was to come.

"Once again I will tell you, Miss Finkle," said Jess sternly, "that you are coming with us now."

"Once again I will ask you," retorted Andromeda, "not to call me by that name again!"

Jess waved the two men forward to detain Andromeda and the others. Andromeda clenched her metal fists tightly, her eyes darting between the two large figures headed her way. She swung one of her fists as hard as she possibly could at one of the men's faces as he reached her. The man reeled around with his face completely missing, as if it were a tub of ice cream with a large scoop missing out of it, and crashed to the ground. Jess, who was watching from behind, gasped at the sight.

The other man stood in shock for a moment but quickly snapped out of it and rushed at Andromeda. Mark dashed between the two of them in a flash. With a swift whip of his hand to the man's throat, Mark sent the man's head flying through the air, and it landed in the gravel beneath their feet. The decapitated body fell to the ground. Andromeda looked at Mark and Audrey in fear and awe as they smiled caringly back at her.

"Go now," said Mark urgently. "We take care of this Jess woman."

Andromeda nodded and rushed toward the hangar, where Turd and the others stood waiting. Mark and Audrey turned around and watched Andromeda as she ran. When they turned back toward Jess, they discovered she was missing.

"Aw, come on," lamented Audrey, slapping her forehead with her hand. "Just like in the movies. We turn around for a second, and the villain gets away in the process!"

"It's just one person," reassured Mark. "She won't get far on foot. She left her car here like idiot. Let's get Andromeda into the air."

They walked briskly into the hangar and reached the airship, where the others were helping Andromeda and Turd onto the cart and into the gondola. Ropes hung from the sides of the ship.

Once Andromeda and Turd were inside the cockpit, they switched on the electronics and gave a thumbs-up to the others outside. Each member of the group took a rope and began to pull the airship forward.

The wheels of the cart creaked and groaned as the craft began to enter the clear night air outside the hangar. The moon came out from behind the clouds and shone its white light on the exterior of the canvas on the airship. Once the entire thing was pulled clear of the hangar, the ropes began to tighten in the hands of the group holding them, and the cart under the gondola started to lift off the ground slightly.

Andromeda opened a window in the cockpit. "All the equipment checks are complete," she said to the others outside. "We are ready for departure."

The group outside, while holding firmly on to the ropes, unhooked the latches that held the gondola to the cart.

"Up ship!" Andromeda called out.

The group slowly let the ropes slide out of their hands as the airship lifted itself into the night sky. Andromeda and Turd looked down at the group of friends where they stood, growing smaller and smaller. They all waved at each other.

"Big moment of truth," said Mark to the others.

"What's that?" asked Avory.

"That that balloon fires up and gets moving," answered Mark.

Andromeda turned on the ignition for the propeller engines. After a brief moment of listening to the old engines sputter, the two pilots jolted when they heard them suddenly spring to life with a loud, roaring buzz!

"And here ... we ... go!" exclaimed Andromeda with a nervous fervor. Turd barked in excitement.

The others on the ground looked up at the large craft as it loomed high above them in the sky. They cheered as it began to slowly cruise forward.

"Goodbye, Andromeda," said Avory, trying to not choke up.

"Aw, Avory," said Betty, patting Avory's shoulder. "She will be back again someday."

"Yes," chimed in Mark. "I will have a way to keep in communication with her. Whenever she get where she is going."

Audrey hugged Mark, then noticed something up in the sky. It looked like the silhouette of a figure dangling from one of the ropes on the airship. "Is that what I think it is?" she asked Mark.

"Yes," answered Mark. "What a dumbass!"

Jess Harper clung to the rope hanging from the airship and hissed in anger as she pulled herself up toward the windows of the cockpit.

"Hey, Doc," mumbled Turd as he looked out the window. "We got company."

"Oh no!" exclaimed Andromeda. "I don't see anything on the radar!"

"You wouldn't," said Turd. "It's right out the window."

Andromeda glanced over at the window, and her eyes widened in disbelief. Outside the window, glaring inside, was Jess, who began to punch the glass.

"You have got to be kidding me," muttered Andromeda, rolling her eyes.

She went over to the window and began to open it. Turd watched in horror as Jess grabbed

Andromeda by the collar and began to pull her out of the window, yanking at her like a lunatic.

"What in the hell are you doing?" yelled Andromeda as she struggled to maintain her balance in the cockpit. "Let me help you inside!"

"You're dead!" hissed Jess, her eyes bloodshot.

"Seriously?" asked Andromeda. "You're crazy. Here, let me help you inside!"

Jess yanked harder on Andromeda's collar, causing Andromeda to slip and fall halfway out of the window. In the process, Jess's grip slipped. Andromeda caught her by the hands and held on tightly. The two hung helplessly out the side of the ship. Turd yelped in fear.

"One last time, you idiot," exclaimed Andromeda, "stop trying to pull me out of the ship and let me get us safely inside!"

"No," snarled Jess. "You're dead, Allison Finkle!"

A sudden rush of adrenaline and anger swept up Andromeda's spine. She wanted to just let go of Jess's hands. She fought this emotion, determined to do what she felt was right and not let her flashes of rage take over. Andromeda managed to wriggle her waist back into the cockpit, using all of her strength to pull up the crazed human at the end of her metal fingertips. After much struggling, Andromeda managed to get Jess up into the window of the cockpit.

"There," sighed Andromeda, breathing heavily. "Now what?"

Jess sat in the window, shaking with adrenaline and insanity. "I'm going to kill you," she muttered under her breath. "I can't let you live. I'm devoted to Omega, and you are preventing us from reaching our goal!"

"No shit, Sherlock," retorted Andromeda. "Omega can rot in hell for all I care."

Jess growled and lunged at Andromeda. As she did so, her foot slipped and she lost her balance. Jess's weak arms and hands were not strong enough to grab on to something to keep her from falling backward out of the cockpit window. Andromeda quickly reached out to try to help her but instead had to watch as Jess fell and disappeared into the clouds below.

"It's all done now," murmured Andromeda, feeling dejected that she had tried to save Jess but couldn't.

Turd whimpered and cuddled up against her leg. "It'll be okay," he whispered. "You did all you could."

Andromeda held the dog tightly to her chest. "All right, Turd," she said, trying to shake the emotions of the moment and move on. "Next stop . . . the island my father mapped out!"

"Aye, aye, Captain!" exclaimed Turd, happily. "New adventures and a new life await us!"

"Yes," smiled Andromeda. "I love you, Turd."

Turd smiled back. "I love you too, Dr. Andromeda Fallout."

## THE END